"YOU DO DANCE?"

"Yes, I dance," Connor replied in a cold voice.

"What of waltzing?"

"If you wish me to waltz, then you have only to teach me."

The riot of color that flooded Portia's face delighted Connor. "I cannot teach you to waltz!" she exclaimed, thoroughly vexed.

"Why not? Are you saying that *you* do not waltz?"

"Of course I waltz!" she snapped. "That is to say, I have learned the dance, but I have never actually performed it."

He gave a pleased nod. "Then we shall learn from each other. When would you like to start?"

Portia opened her mouth to continue arguing, but realized the wretch had outmaneuvered her. There was no way she could insist he learn to dance if she did not follow suit. "You are enjoying this, aren't you?" she accused.

"Not yet, my dear," he drawled, his green eyes dancing. "But I will."

A PROPER TAMING

JOAN OVERFIELD

AVON BOOKS NEW YORK

A PROPER TAMING is an original publication of Avon Books. This
work has never before appeared in book form. This work is a novel.
Any similarity to actual persons or events is purely coincidental.

AVON BOOKS
A division of
The Hearst Corporation
1350 Avenue of the Americas
New York, New York 10019

First Avon Books Printing: August 1994

AVON TRADEMARK REG. U.S. PAT. OFF. AND IN OTHER COUNTRIES, MARCA
REGISTRADA, HECHO EN U.S.A.

Printed in the U.S.A.

RA 10 9 8 7 6 5 4 3 2 1

1

Sheffield, England, 1817

It was not that she was one of those ladies who went about engaging in fits of the vapors. Indeed, Miss Portia Haverall had always held such creatures in quiet contempt, and had vowed never to emulate them. But after the events of the past year, she was beginning to wonder if it was time to reconsider the matter. Surely one small swoon would not compromise her lofty principles, she thought, glaring at the butler who was blocking her path. A moment later, she angrily shook off the impulse.

"What do you mean her ladyship is not here?" she demanded, lifting the black veil covering her face to better see her elderly opponent. "I wrote my great-aunt I was coming!"

"I am sure you did, Miss . . . Haverall, is it not?" the majordomo said, his tone condescending as he studied her down the length of his nose. "However, your missive, if indeed you sent one, appears to have gone astray. Nor do I recall the countess mentioning she was expecting company, as she surely would have done. Perhaps you have the wrong address?" he added with a superior smirk that set Portia's teeth on edge.

For a moment she contemplated the pleasure it

1

would give her to bring her reticule down on the
butler's balding head, but she was too weary to
make the attempt. The journey from her village
near London in the Cotswolds, which should have
taken two days at the most, had taken closer to
four, and she was at the end of her endurance.
First her rented carriage lost its wheel, then the
lead horse had gone lame, and as if that were not
bad enough, the drink-sodden driver she had foolishly engaged had managed to get them going
south rather than north.

She was exhausted, aching from the constant
bouncing, and she wanted nothing more than to
collapse on the nearest bed and sleep for a week.
Unfortunately, it seemed even these simple luxu-
ries would be denied her by a fate which had
proven capricious of late. Fighting back the re-
newed desire to give in to the vapors, she raised
her face until her gray eyes met the butler's suspicious gaze.

"If you would be so good as to tell me where
her ladyship has gone, I would like to send her a
note," she said haughtily, clinging to the frayed
edges of her composure with grim determination.

The butler hesitated, then said, "Lady Lowton is
in Scotland to attend the birth of her grandchild. I
have no idea when she may return."

"She has gone to Edinburgh?" Portia exclaimed
in dismay, the hope that her aunt was enjoying a
mere weekend in the country vanishing.

The fact that Portia knew her ladyship's oldest
son lived in Edinburgh seemed to relieve the elderly butler of some of his reservations, although
he still showed a marked reluctance to let Portia
inside.

"Yes, Miss Haverall," he replied, his tone not
quite so supercilious. "She is residing with the earl
and his lady on Charlotte Square. If you like, I

would be happy to forward your message for you. Will you be staying in Sheffield?"

From this Portia surmised that staying in the elegant manor house was out of the question, and she bit back an angry retort. "If you could recommend a respectable inn, I will be staying," she said, her mind already turning to the difficulty of an unescorted female remaining at a public inn. She had engaged a companion to accompany her from Chipping Campden, but she wasn't sure she could convince the older lady to remain for an indefinite time.

"The Red Dove is considered fashionable, and I am sure you shall be comfortable there," the butler offered hesitantly, clearly uncertain what to do. "I should allow you to stay here had her ladyship left instructions to that effect, but as it is . . ." His voice trailed off and he gave a helpless shrug.

Portia sensed he was weakening, and toyed with the idea of pressing her advantage. In the end, however, she decided the effort was not worth the candle, and accepted the inevitable with a weary sigh. "That is all right. I understand you can not admit me without permission," she said quietly, resisting the urge to connive her way past him.

"If you have need, I will send a maid along to attend you," the butler said, apparently anxious to offer what assistance he could. "It would not do for a member of the countess's family to be attended by a common maid from an inn."

Whereas it would apparently "do" for a member of her ladyship's family to stay at that same inn, Portia thought with a flash of her usual irreverence. "That is not necessary, sir. I brought my own maid with me." she said, raising her chin to give the man a mocking smile. "But I do thank you for the kind offer," she added, her tone fairly dripping with sarcasm. She then turned and stalked back to the waiting carriage.

"Well, what is it?" her companion, Mrs. Quincy, demanded, her black eyes full of distrust as Portia climbed inside. "Your great-aunt refuse to see you? I'm not surprised; you likely offended her sensibilities by arriving in a rented hack. The gentry's queer that way, did I not warn you?"

"Indeed you did, Mrs. Quincy, a dozen times at least," Portia replied, closing her eyes and collapsing against the cushions with a heavy sigh. After spending four days trapped inside the cramped conveyance with Mrs. Quincy, Portia did not know what she feared more—that the older woman with her rigid sensibilities and a tongue that dripped acid would refuse to stay with her another day, or that she would agree.

"What is amiss?" Mrs. Quincy prodded, her brows meeting in a scowl. "If your aunt isn't refusing you the door, why are you still here? We're not lost again, are we?"

"No, we are not lost, nor has my aunt refused me admittance," Portia replied, gritting her teeth as she fought to remain civil. "It seems her ladyship has gone to Edinburgh for a visit, and since she left no instructions to the contrary, the staff cannot let me stay in the house. We shall have to put up at an inn until I contact my aunt."

"We?" Mrs. Quincy's expression grew even more sour.

Portia clenched her hands in her lap. "I was hoping you would be gracious enough to remain with me," she said, mentally cursing the necessity for such an arrangement. "I have Nancy with me, of course, but I feel it might look better if I was properly chaperoned."

"I should think so," Mrs. Quincy opined with a loud sniff, giving the middle-aged maid sitting beside Portia a baleful glare. "Bad enough that an unmarried female should stay at a public inn in the first place, but to stay with only a simple maid to lend you countenance ..." Her massive frame shook with horror. "Well, I am sure I need not tell you what people would think about *that*."

Pompous old hag, Portia thought, although she managed to keep her expression blank. "Then you will stay?"

Mrs. Quincy drew herself up rigidly. "I should hope I know my Christian duty as well as the next woman, Miss Haverall. I would never dream of leaving a fellow sister in danger of jeopardizing her virtue and her good name. You may rely upon me to remain so long as I am needed."

With that hurdle behind her, Portia was able to scrape up a tired smile. "Thank you, ma'am. That is most gracious of you."

"Of course," the other woman added, a sly look in her dark eyes, "I was paid to accompany you only as far as Sheffield. I had planned to return home on the next mail coach, as I have another position waiting for me. But naturally I shan't give such paltry financial considerations another thought."

Perhaps she wouldn't be eternally damned if she should accidentally kick the old witch's shins, Portia thought, wistfully studying Mrs. Quincy's bombazine-draped limbs. She had but to uncross her ankles and ...

"I should be more than happy to reimburse you for the inconvenience, Mrs. Quincy," she said instead, mentally admonishing herself for the lapse in control. "Another ten pounds, shall we say?"

"I would have made fifteen at the other post." Mrs. Quincy's prompt reply told Portia she had been unwisely generous in her initial offer.

"Fifteen, then," Portia agreed, then uncrossed

her ankles, allowing the toe of her kid half-boots to come into painful contact with Mrs. Quincy's thick ankles.

"Ouch!"

"Did I kick you?" Portia's eyes were wide with innocence. "Oh, dear, how very clumsy of me. I am sorry."

"Sour-faced, mean-spirited, money-grubbing old witch!" Nancy muttered, her jaw clenching with fury as she flung Portia's belongings into the small wardrobe that came with the simply furnished room. "I vow, that one could tell vinegar how to be bitter! Whyever did you hire the harpy in the first place? Your wits must have gone begging, is what."

"Please, Nancy, no more, I implore you." Portia groaned, pressing the washcloth dipped in lavender water to her throbbing temples. "My poor head feels as if it is about to split open."

"And small wonder, I shouldn't think," Nancy grumbled, although she lowered her voice. "Four days with that female could give a statue a case of the colic! And as for you ... well, all I can say is 'tis a good thing your father wasn't here to see you. He'd have thought you dicked in the nob for sure."

Portia opened one eye to give the maid an indignant glare. "Me? I have been a pattern card of propriety!"

"That's what I mean." Nancy placed her hands on her hips and fixed Portia with an accusing look. "Since when would you have put up with that female's nonsense for more than five minutes, hmm? I could hardly credit my own eyes and ears the way you kept casting down your eyes and simpering like a green school-miss." She shook her head in obvious disgust.

"I never simpered!" Portia denied, eyes flashing at the hateful accusation.

"And you didn't put Mrs. Quincy in her place as you ought to have done, either!" Nancy was merciless in her summation of Portia's behavior. "Whatever ails you, girl? You've never acted like such a ninnyhammer in the past."

The querulous comment from someone who had known Portia since she was in short frocks drove out her anger, and Portia collapsed back on the uncomfortable bed. She remained silent for a long moment, struggling to find the words that would explain the abrupt change in her manners.

"Perhaps I am tired of playing the vixen," she said at last, her expression troubled as she gazed down at her clenched hands. "I have been thinking, and I've concluded that 'tis my own fault Papa disinherited me. If I hadn't acted like such a willful child, he would never have cut me out of his will."

"But he was always disinheriting you!" Nancy protested in alarm. "He cut you out of his will at least four times a year, only to put you back in once his temper was cooled. Even Mr. Clinden's solicitors admitted he'd have doubtlessly put you back in that last time, except . . ."

"Except that he died before he had the chance," Portia finished when Nancy's voice trailed off. "I know, but that is precisely the point. If I hadn't squabbled and disagreed with Papa over every little thing, he wouldn't have needed to disinherit me at all."

"But—"

"Don't you see?" Portia interrupted, raising anguished eyes to meet Nancy's gaze. "Papa had every right to disinherit me! I failed him as a daughter, and I do not deserve to be his heir."

Nancy's jaw dropped in shock. "You can't believe that," she managed at last, twisting her work-worn hands in dismay. "Your father loved you!"

"And I loved him." This time Portia made no attempt to blink back the tears scalding her eyes. "He was the dearest father anyone could want, and I shall miss him always. But toward the end, I knew I had disappointed him. He wanted a sweet-tempered, well-behaved daughter, and he got me instead."

"Oh, pet." Nancy hurried over to sit beside her. "You mustn't think such sad thoughts! Disappointed in you? Why, your father was proud as proud could be of you! Many were the times he would say to me, 'Nancy, that daughter of mine would invade hades and tell the devil himself how to manage purgatory.' Now, does that sound like he was ashamed of you?"

Secretly, Portia thought that it did. She also recalled her papa saying the same thing to her, but looking back she wondered if her father was condemning her independent and willful ways, rather than praising them. Toward the end he had chastised her for what he termed her "unfeminine nature," and had begun urging her to consider her cousin Reginald's offer of marriage. At the time she'd thought he was simply trying to provoke her. Now she wasn't so sure.

" 'Tis your nerves, that's what," Nancy decided, giving Portia's hand a brisk pat and bustling her under the covers. "And after the year you've had, 'tis no small wonder. First your poor father dying so sudden-like, and then that awful court battle to have his will overturned. I shouldn't doubt but that you're all out of curl. You just rest for a bit, and you'll soon be feeling your old self again. You'll see."

Portia dutifully closed her eyes, but as soon as

she heard the door closing behind Nancy, she opened them again. *My old self,* she thought bitterly, turning on her side. A fat lot of good her old self had ever done anyone.

She had barreled through life, behaving as outrageously as she pleased with no thought to the consequences. Even her squabbles with Papa, which had resulted in her being disinherited, had seemed a game. She'd loved provoking him, and she'd have sworn he'd enjoyed their spats with equal relish. Hadn't he been the one to teach her to use her own mind, and never to bow to any man?

But if that was true, she told herself, then why couldn't she shake the terrible feeling that she had disappointed him? Their last quarrel, caused by her refusal to consider her tiresome cousin's yearly offer of marriage, had been their most bitter, and the memory of it still hurt her deeply.

Reginald had come up from London for his annual visit, and as was his custom, he'd proposed. She'd refused, as she always did, and Reginald had returned to his home in the city. She'd thought that the end of it, until her father shocked her by hinting that marriage to Reginald, who was both a fop and a fool, might not be such a terrible fate after all.

"The lad merely wants guidance," he had insisted, glowering at her over the rim of his spectacles. "And you know there's nothing you'd relish more than leading some man about by the nose. The two of you are well-suited."

She'd replied tartly that the only place Reginald was likely to want guiding was to the nearest tailor, and the battle was joined. The more her father pressed the match, the more obstreperous she became. When her father disinherited her in his usual dramatic fashion, she retaliated by threaten-

ing to run off and become a governess. They were
still at daggers drawn when, three days later, he
passed away quietly in his sleep.

That was what hurt most, she admitted, shifting
restlessly beneath the thin blankets. Her father had
died thinking her a failure, a sad disappointment
to him because of her sharp tongue and willful
ways. The last thing he had said to her on the
night he died was that for once in his life, he
would like to see her behave as a lady should.
Now he was gone, and she was left to wonder if
her pride and outspoken manner were worth the
price she was now paying.

Well, no more, she decided, swiping at her tears.
She had tried playing the stubborn shrew, and
only look where it had landed her. From this day
forward she would be the lady her father had
wanted her to be. She would be demure, well-
behaved, and, above all else, she would hold her
wretched tongue, regardless of the provocation.
She had already made a good start of it, she
mused, thinking of Mrs. Quincy. If she had managed to control both her temper and her tongue
around that nagging female, then she could do
anything. The thought cheered her, and she closed
her eyes, sliding easily into a deep, peaceful sleep.

At first Portia thought the loud pounding on the
door of her room was part of her fitful dream, and
she snuggled deeper into the pillows. She was on
the verge of drifting off again when a female
scream sent her bolt upright in bed. What on
earth? she wondered, shaking off sleep as she
stared groggily about her. Then the screaming and
pounding started again.

"The beast! The beast! Someone save me from
the beast!"

The terror in the voice had Portia scrambling

out of bed, pulling on her night robe as she raced for the door. With no thought for her own safety, she fumbled with the bolt and threw open the heavy door.

"What is going on?" she snapped irritably, blinking at the petite blonde who was standing in front of her door. "What are you caterwauling about at this unseemly hour?"

Wasting no time with explanations, the blonde pushed herself past Portia and into the room.

"Oh, please, dear madam, close the door, I beg of you!" she cried, her blue eyes wide with fear as she pressed her back to the far wall. "He is after me!"

"Who is after you? Your husband?" Portia demanded, although she did as she was asked. She'd heard of men who brutally used their wives, and wondered if the poor girl was afflicted with such a creature. If so, she'd give the wretch a tongue-lashing he'd not soon forget, she decided, her vow to be a lady forgotten as her lips thinned with anger.

The blonde shook her head, causing her golden curls to dance about her delicate face. "It is the . . . the beast!" she stammered, her voice quavering with dread. "I had heard he was fearsome, but he is an earl, after all, and I thought . . . Oh!" She buried her face in her hands. "I cannot go through with this! I wish to go home!"

It suddenly occurred to Portia that the pretty blonde, for all she was well-spoken, might be a doxy who'd had a falling-out with her protector. She also knew that a true lady of breeding such as herself should faint dead away at being faced with such an untenable situation, but her logical self argued that such behavior would be a colossal waste of time. Instead she turned her mind to helping the fear-stricken young woman.

"What did the beast do?" she asked, steeling herself to hear the worst. "Did he . . . er . . . assault you?"

The pretty blonde shook her head, her cheeks turning a delicate rose. "Oh, no, it was nothing like that! He has been a gentleman in *that* respect, but this is not at all what I was expecting when I agreed to go with him. He is so cold, so overpowering, that I vow I am in terror of him!" She raised tear-filled blue eyes to Portia's face. "Oh, you must help me escape him, ma'am!" she sobbed piteously. "You must!"

Portia hesitated, certain there must be more to the story than the pretty blonde was admitting to. As far as she could tell, "the beast," whoever he might be, had done nothing untoward. And yet why else would the young woman have fled into the night to escape him? Ah, well, Portia thought, giving a mental shrug, she supposed it did not matter.

"Have you money to secure passage home?" she asked, reaching a swift decision. While she was not an heiress, she felt her pockets were sufficiently plump to lend whatever assistance was required. Even if she had not had much money, she could hardly turn her back on the terrified creature standing before her. She had been raised to do her duty toward those in need, and clearly the young lady qualified on that account.

"Y-yes." The blonde gave an unhappy sniff. "But my bags are in the room his lordship arranged for me, and I dare not go back there! What if he should take me captive?"

Portia remained silent, considering the ramifications of any action she might take. She knew the wisest thing would be to summon the innkeeper and let him deal with the matter, but she quickly discarded the notion. For all she knew, the man could be in league with this "beast," and would only deliver the woman back into his lordship's vile clutches the moment her back was turned.

"You may stay in my room for the night," Portia said, arriving at what she deemed the only possible solution. "In the morning, I shall send one of the maids to collect your things."

"Oh, ma'am!" Blue eyes filled with tears as the blonde clasped her hands together. "Thank you! You have saved me! How shall I ever repay you for your kindness?"

The heartfelt words made Portia wonder if she had mistaken the situation. Granted her knowledge of such things was practically nonexistent, but she much doubted a prostitute would have expressed such ardent thanks for being saved from a patron. She was about to renew her request for an explanation when a second bout of pounding on her door drowned out the rest of her thoughts.

"Miss Montgomery?" a deep male voice called out in obvious irritation. "Are you in there?"

"It is the beast!" the blonde shrieked, glancing wildly about her for a place to hide. "He has found me!"

"Blast it, ma'am, will you stop enacting a Cheltenham tragedy over this? Open this door at once!" the man demanded with what Portia regarded as unbelievable arrogance. She was about to call out for assistance when the latch rattled ominously, and she realized in horror that she had neglected to lock it.

Quickly she sought a weapon, her gaze falling on the long-handled brass bed warmer hanging by the hearth. She snatched it up in shaking hands, and whirled about to face the door just as it was thrust open. A very large, very fierce-looking man stood on the threshold, his black brows gathered in a scowl as he glared at the blonde pressed against the wall.

"Miss Montgomery," he began, his voice clipped as he moved further into the room, "how many times must I explain that it is my mother who has engaged your services? I am but escorting you to her, and I assure you that I have no designs on your virtue. Now kindly return to your room; you are being tiresome."

"No!" the blonde exclaimed, continuing to cower in obvious fright. "Stay away from me, I shan't go with you! I shan't!"

The gentleman's green eyes narrowed with fury as he advanced inexorably toward his prey. "I warn you, ma'am, I am beginning to lose my patience with you," he said, his voice soft with menace. "If you do not come with me this very moment, I vow you shall have cause to regret it."

Portia had had enough of such blatant bullying. She stepped forward, raising the heavy bed warmer high above her head and then bringing it down with all her might. The blow connected solidly with the back of the intruder's head, bringing him crashing down like a felled tree.

The sight apparently proved too much for Miss Montgomery's sensibilities, for she uttered a piercing shriek and collapsed in a dead faint. Portia stared at her in dismay, her gaze moving from her crumpled form to that of the man she knew only as "the beast." Now what? she wondered, but before she could decide upon a course of action, her room was suddenly filled with strangers, all milling about and offering advice and admonishments in increasingly loud voices.

The commotion brought the innkeeper, clad in a faded night robe, querulously demanding what the devil was going on. Portia was about to oblige him when he caught sight of the unconscious man lying on the floor.

"Good Lord love us!" he exclaimed, his voice so weak that Portia wondered if he was about to faint as well. "Ye've just killed the bloody earl!"

2

Connor Dewhurst, sixth earl of Doncaster, groaned at the pain throbbing in his head in rhythm with the beating of his heart. He must be as jug-bitten as a duke, and he stoically decided the discomfort he was experiencing was apt punishment for his sins. The odd thing was, he couldn't remember drinking a single glass of port, let alone the amount of spirits it would have taken to reduce him to this state. In fact, he realized, fighting against pain and panic, he couldn't remember anything at all! The acknowledgement startled him out of the black fog that filled his mind, and he struggled to focus his hazy thoughts.

The first thing he realized was that he was lying on the floor, and there was evidently a small riot raging above him. Several people were all shouting at once. It required all of his concentration to separate the voices so that he could make sense of them.

" . . . in all my life!" he heard a woman exclaiming, outrage clearly evident in her sharp tones. "You, missy, are naught but a hoyden, and I wonder I should ever have been deceived by your simpering ways! I shouldn't remain with you now were you to offer me all the gold in Prinny's pocket!"

"Considering the paltry sum that would amount

to, Mrs. Quincy, I fear you are selling your services rather cheaply." He heard another woman— younger, judging from the sound of her voice— respond tartly, and he suppressed a grin at her cutting wit. It was just the sort of thing his mother would say, and he hoped he would remember it so that he might repeat it to her once he returned to Hawkshurst.

"We'll have to have the constable in." A man's whining voice rose above the others. "His lordship is a man of great power, and there's no telling what he'll do once he comes to his senses. He'll have us all transported, I'll be bound."

Connor wondered why he would desire to have anyone transported, but everything seemed such a muddle. Memory was slowly returning. He could vaguely remember arriving at an inn with his mother's newest companion. He'd met the tiresome creature in Cambridge and was escorting her back to his estate in Yorkshire per his mother's request.

The lady—Miss Montgomery, his addled brain provided—had seemed pleased with the situation at first, and had done everything within her power to fix his interest. But when he'd made it obvious that he wasn't taken with her, she'd withdrawn into silence, casting him nervous glances as if he was a cossack out on a rampage.

It was a reaction to which, over the years, he had become inured, especially from the fairer sex, and he'd ignored her inexplicable fear of him. He'd been preparing for bed when the maid he'd brought with him to act as chaperone had tapped on his door and announced Miss Montgomery had fled into the night. Disgusted, and more than a little concerned for her safety, he'd given chase, vowing to send her back to Cambridge on the next coach when he found her. His search had proven fruitless, and he'd been about to return to his rooms and summon the innkeeper when he saw a door closing down the hall. He remembered knocking on the door, asking for Miss Montgomery, and then . . .

"You hit me!' he exclaimed, his eyes flying open. He closed them almost immediately, muttering curses at the white-hot pain that exploded behind his eyes.

"Well, of course I hit you, you miscreant," he heard the younger woman say. "You were about to attack Miss Montgomery."

The accusation made Connor open his eyes again, albeit somewhat cautiously, and he fixed the speaker with a blurry glare. It took a moment for her features to come into focus, and he found himself gazing at a female he had never seen in his life.

That she was tall he noted first. That she was well-formed and possessed of a delicate beauty he noticed second. He took the time to admire her dark curls and silver-colored eyes before he fixed her with a furious glare. "Who the devil are you?" he demanded, wondering if he could sit up without casting up his accounts.

"I am Miss Portia Haverall," the woman said, drawing herself up proudly, her smokey eyes sparkling with defiance as she returned his glare. "And if you think you can have me transported, you may think again! My great-aunt is the Dowager Countess of Lowton, and I assure you she is not without influence in this village!"

"You may consider me cowed, Miss Haverall," Connor retorted sarcastically, cautiously raising himself on an elbow. The room was still dipping and spinning, but at least he no longer felt in danger of losing his dinner. He raised his other hand to the side of his head and winced as he fingered the large lump forming there. At least he wasn't bleeding, he mused, taking from that thought what small comfort he could.

"Are you all right, my lord?" The innkeeper, a short, plump man with anxious eyes, shouldered his way past the woman who had identified herself as Miss Haverall. He wrung his hands as he stared down at Connor. "I've sent for Dr. Crowley, and I can have the constable here in a thrice if you'd like."

Connor's gaze flashed back to Miss Haverall's face. Despite her defiant words he saw the apprehension in her proud expression, and the nervous way she nibbled her lips. He admired their lush ripeness, and then carefully shook his head.

"The constable may enjoy his sleep," he said, pushing himself into a sitting position. "I see no reason to disturb him . . . yet." He glanced about him. "Where is Miss Montgomery?"

"If you are referring to that poor child you were attempting to assault, she is not here." Miss Haverall's smile was dangerously close to smug. "And you ought to be ashamed of yourself for forcing your attentions on such a gently bred young lady!"

Connor's hand dropped to his side, his temper flaming to life. "That is the second time you have accused me of dishonoring my name and my title," he said, his voice soft with menace as he sought to gain control. "I don't suggest you do it a third time."

He saw her bite her lip again, but at least she remained silent. He gazed at her for another long moment, blinking as he suddenly noted she was in her night robe. Indeed, he realized, glancing about him with dawning comprehension, everyone, including the apologetic innkeeper, was dressed for bed. His eyebrows met in a dark scowl as the implications of his presence in a lady's bedchamber occurred to him.

"Just what sort of rig are you running here?" he demanded, his jaw clenching as he turned a furious gaze on Miss Haverall. "Why did Miss Montgomery run to *you*? If I find you are in league with her—"

If he'd thought to offend or intimidate Miss Haverall with his accusations, it was obvious he had underestimated his opponent. Instead of cowering with fear or erupting with self-righteous indignation, she simply tossed back her tumbled dark curls and fixed him with a glare that could have frozen an inferno.

"If you think I would willingly lure you into my bedchamber, you doltish beast, then 'tis plain the blow to your head has affected the few wits you possess!" She regally ignored the dismayed gasps that followed her pronouncement. "Now kindly leave my room. You may await the doctor elsewhere."

Connor's lips tightened, and he considered letting his ferocious temper slip. He couldn't remember the last time anyone had given him such a dressing-down, and only the risk of scandal prevented him from telling the little shrew what he thought of her. For the moment he knew he had no choice but to quit the field, and it stung his considerable pride. If it was the last thing he did, he vowed, he would make her pay for the insults she had hurled at him.

"As you say, Miss Haverall," he said, motioning the innkeeper for assistance. The smaller man rushed forward, slipping his arms beneath Connor's shoulder and levering him to his feet. It took some effort and a great deal of grunting, but Connor was finally standing. He took a few deep breaths to combat the dizziness, and, when he was sure he wouldn't collapse, he drew himself up to his full, intimidating height.

"Do not think this is the end of the matter, ma'am," he informed her, making each word drip with menace. "I shall expect to discuss this with you first thing tomorrow morning. And if you are thinking about sneaking away, I shouldn't advise it. Your great-aunt might be the Dowager Countess of Lowton, but I am the Earl of Doncaster. Attempt to leave here, and you will learn of the power I command in this village. Do you understand?"

Miss Haverall's cheeks flushed with temper, but she remained civil. "Yes, my lord," she said in a tight voice.

"Good." He allowed himself a cool nod, and with the innkeeper's stammering apologies filling his ears, he made his way to his rooms.

"Well, I hope you are satisfied!" The door had scarce closed behind the earl before Mrs. Quincy was letting her displeasure be known. "Disgrace and ruin, that is what you have brought down on all our heads! We shall be taken up over this, you mark my words, and if you think I mean to suffer for *your* folly, you are all about in the head! I shall inform his lordship I had nothing to do with this . . . this display, and then I shall return to Chipping Campden where you may make very sure I shall waste no time in informing the vicar of your conduct. Not that it should surprise him in the slightest," she added with a sneer. "He warned me you were a limb of Satan. Would that I had listened!"

"And would that I had listened to my solicitor, Mrs. Quincy. He told me you were a shrew of the first water, and it would appear he did not lie," Portia retorted, wearily rubbing her forehead.

Now that the initial excitement had faded, she was feeling oddly flat, and the only thing she desired was privacy in which to soothe her lacerated nerves. Unfortunately it appeared she would have to do battle if she hoped to enjoy even that small courtesy.

Mrs. Quincy's jaw dropped at the sharp words. Her mouth opened and closed several times before she managed a strangled, "Well, of all the ungrateful, ill-mannered females it has been my misfortune to encounter! You, Miss Haverall, are naught but a hussy, and you may consider our association at an end! Good night!" And she stormed out of the room, her hooked nose held high in the air.

"And good riddance to you, you old cat!" Nancy responded, closing the door with a satisfying bang. She turned back to Portia with a look of grim delight. "If I'd known that smashing a bed warmer over a lord's head was all it took to be shed of that biddy, I'd have done it myself days ago! Now mayhap we can enjoy some peace and quiet without listening to her snipping and complaining every five minutes."

Portia's lips curved in a reluctant smile. "Doubtlessly that is what Dryden meant about everything being good for something," she said. Then her smile faded as the reality of their situation set in. "Nancy, you don't think his lordship will have me arrested, do you?"

The maid's expression grew as somber as her mistress's. "As to that, miss, there's no way of telling," she said, nervously clasping her hands together. "He did seem a trifle put out with you, but mayhap he'll be in better fiddle once his head ain't paining him. And don't be forgetting it's *him* as pushed his way into *your* bedchamber. No judge is likely to fault you for protecting yourself however you could."

Her words eased some of Portia's fears as she considered that aspect of the matter. "There is that," she agreed slowly, her lips curving in a thoughtful smile as she imagined how she would defend herself should the earl drag her in front of a magistrate. She'd wear her primmest gown, she decided, presenting herself as a well-connected lady of respectable birth forced by unhappy circumstances to spend the night at an inn. Naturally, she would tearfully assure an understanding judge, when a strange man barged into her room she did the only thing possible in the circumstances.

Perhaps she'd even mention her father's death, she mused, brightening at the possibility. Any judge worthy of the name was certain to look more kindly upon an orphan who ... Her thoughts slammed to a horrified halt as she realized the direction they had taken. She was doing it again, plotting and scheming so that she might have her own way. And to compound her crime, she was even planning to use her father's death to justify her actions ... She closed her eyes as bitter guilt burned through her.

"Miss Portia, are you all right?" Nancy was regarding her anxiously. "You've gone as white as a corpse!"

"I'm just tired, that is all," Portia replied, not wishing to share her dark thoughts with anyone, not even Nancy. "If you'll excuse me, I believe I shall try to get back to sleep. I daresay I shall be needing my rest come the morrow."

"Aye, that's the truth of it," Nancy agreed darkly, bustling forward to assist her into bed. "Although how you'll be getting any sleep after all of this, I'm sure I don't know. That reminds me. Where's the young lady what started the commotion? I've not so much as caught a glimpse of her."

"I'm not sure," Portia admitted, frowning as she realized she hadn't given Miss Montgomery more than a passing thought since she'd smashed the earl over the head. Somehow in the middle of all the commotion Miss Montgomery had managed to slip away.

"Ah, well, doubtlessly she'll turn up for breakfast." Nancy dismissed the unknown woman with an indifferent shrug. "You just close your eyes, sweeting, and try to get some rest. You'll be wanting to look your best when you face his lordship again."

Portia smiled sleepily at the maid's endearment. "You haven't called me that in years," she said, exhaustion pulling at her.

"Haven't I?" Nancy tugged the covers up to Portia's chin.

"Maybe it's because I haven't been particularly sweet," Portia mumbled around a yawn, her eyes drifting closed as she snuggled against the pillow. "Good night, Nancy."

"What do you mean she isn't here?" Connor roared, then winced as his head began throbbing anew. He cursed roundly beneath his breath, and then spoke again, his voice carefully modulated. "How did she get away?" he asked, fixing the maid with a baleful glare. "I thought I brought you along to keep an eye on her."

"And so you did," the maid, Gwynnen, replied calmly, apparently unperturbed by her employer's black displeasure. "But even maids must rest, and the little minx stole out while I was sleeping. Took her bags as well, so I reckon we needn't bother looking for her. She's probably halfway back to Cambridge by now."

Connor felt a stab of guilt at the maid's words. "I didn't mean to imply you'd been neglectful," he

muttered, his eyes closing as he pinched the
bridge of his nose. His head was still pounding
like the wrath of God, although that was no doubt
due more to the vile potion the physician had
forced upon him than to the blow. He hadn't felt
so wretched since his early days at Oxford, and he
prayed it was another dozen years before he felt
so poorly again.

"This is all my mother's fault," he announced,
his hand dropping to his side as he met the maid's
gaze. "Why couldn't she just send for this companion like she did all the rest? Why must I come
fetch her?"

Gwynnen's eyes took on a knowing gleam,
which would have alerted Connor had he been in
any shape to take note. "Miss Montgomery's the
great-niece to a viscount," she said, her mouth
pursing in a disapproving line. "Can't expect her
to take the mail coach like a parlor maid."

"I don't see why not," Connor complained, not
yet ready to forgive his mother for the trouble
he had endured. He'd been in the middle of the
lambing season when his mother had insisted he
travel southward to meet her newly hired companion. He'd refused at first, citing his many re-
sponsibilities, but his mother had looked so
downcast and alone that he'd finally given in
with ill grace. Now it appeared his efforts were
all for naught.

"I suppose I shall have to return to Cambridge
and hire some other female for Mother," he grumbled, feeling decidedly put out at the prospect.
"Unless you think we might find someone suitable
here?" His dark spirits lifted in hope.

Gwynnen hesitated. "I reckon we could ask
about," she said, the doubt in her voice making it
plain she thought it unlikely. "Her ladyship's par-

ticular in her notions, and you can't hire just anyone. Although . . ."

"Although what?"

"That young lady, Miss Haverall, is a pretty
thing, don't you think?"

Connor's brows met in a scowl at the mention
of the hell cat who had floored him last night.
"How the devil am I to know?" he snarled, although he remembered a pair of rain-gray eyes
lavishly trimmed with thick, black lashes and a
riot of dark curls cascading from beneath a night-
cap. "The blasted female smashed a bed warmer
over my head before I had a chance to say hello."

"Shows she's a quick thinker." Gwynnen defended the other woman's actions with an approv-
ing nod. "The countess would like that. She don't
like empty-headed females."

"Then she would have been sorely disappointed
with Miss Montgomery," Connor observed with a
singular lack of charity. "The chit was a pea-
goose."

"But so pretty." Gwynnen gave a heavy sigh.
"Just like a little doll, she was."

Connor said nothing, although the maid had
confirmed what he had long suspected. He'd
noted that his mother's main requirement in her
companions was physical beauty, and he'd surmised she was hoping he'd take one look at one of
them and fall head over heels in love. His lips
twisted in a sneer at the possibility. At least a companion would be suitably grateful should he offer,
he thought, bitterly recalling his one Season in
London. God knew not even the temptation of his
wealth and title had been enough to convince a
lady of his own class to accept him.

"My lord!" The impatience in Gwynnen's voice
made it obvious she'd been attempting to get his
attention without success.

"I'm sorry, Gwynnen," Connor apologized, pushing the unhappy memories from his mind. "What is it?"

"I was saying that you might at least speak with Miss Haverall," the maid said with the bluntness of a long-time servant. "Mayhap she would consider the position."

"The niece of the Dowager Countess of Lowton?" Connor asked, recalling Miss Haverall's haughty boast. "I shouldn't think it likely. Besides, I don't want to give her another opportunity to dash in my brains. She did enough damage last night." He fingered the lump on his head.

"Provided she *is* the countess's niece," Gwynnen said, ignoring the rest of Connor's complaint.

Connor raised his head. "Do you think she is not?" he asked, frowning.

Gwynnen shrugged. "The innkeeper told me the countess has a town house in the village. Stands to reason that if Miss Haverall was related to her, she'd be staying there."

He considered the possibility and decided Gwynnen was probably right; a countess was highly unlikely to allow her niece to stay in a public inn. On the other hand, there was something in Miss Haverall's regal bearing that made him believe she was telling the truth.

Perhaps it was her carriage, he mused, remembering the slim, delicate body that had managed to look inviting despite the prim robe covering her from head to foot. And then there was the arrogant way she had tilted her chin up at him, as if inviting him to do his worst. He smiled as he recalled her fiery defiance, and the way she had ripped up at him. Yes, he thought with a cool nod, she was just the sort of companion his mother would like.

"I suppose I could have a word with her," he said coming to an abrupt decision. "What harm could it do?"

Portia spent most of the morning preparing herself for her confrontation with the earl. After a great deal of thought she decided it would be best if she were to appear coolly penitent and remorseful, but not fearful. She would apologize to his lordship for what was really no more than a slight misunderstanding, and as a gentleman, he would have no choice but to accept. After all, as Nancy had wisely pointed out, *he* was the one who had barged into *her* room, and not refining too nicely on the point, he would ultimately be the one who would have far more explaining to do to the authorities than she did.

Mrs. Quincy had made good her threat, departing in high dudgeon on the southbound mail coach. Miss Montgomery had fled on the same coach, and Portia wished them joy of each other.

When the inn's saucy maid came to her rooms to inform her that " 'is lor'ship" was waiting for her in the private parlor, Portia hid her trepidation behind a demure expression. She was wearing a dress of dove-gray merino, trimmed with lavender and black ribbons at the hem and throat, and she was cynically aware that the modestly cut gown showed her to her best advantage. If the earl should tumble to the fact that she was in mourning and decide to take pity on her ... Well, she assured herself with a last look in the cheval glass, that would hardly be *her* fault.

The first thing she noted when she stepped into the cramped parlor which had been set aside for the earl's use was the extravagant fire blazing in the sooty grate. When she'd bespoken the same room last night, it had taken a hefty bribe to obtain even an indifferent fire of wet coal. Evidently the toadying innkeeper considered only an earl to be worthy of a fire of seasoned wood, she mused, sniffing in disapproval.

"Kindly close the door, Miss Haverall, unless you relish having the entire town made privy to our conversation," a cold voice sounded from her right, and Portia turned as the earl rose to his feet.

The apologetic greeting she had been about to utter withered on Portia's lips, and her jaw dropped as the earl advanced toward her. Good heavens! she thought in disbelief. The man was a veritable Goliath!

Dressed in an unfashionably cut jacket of blue velvet that seemed scarce able to contain his broad shoulders, his jet-black hair caught back in an equally unfashionable queue, the earl was quite unlike any other man Portia had ever seen. His height she remembered from last night, but in all the excitement she had somehow overlooked his powerful, muscular physique. An obvious error on her part, she thought, swallowing nervously as he towered over her. For a moment she gave careful consideration to turning tail and fleeing from him as Miss Montgomery had done last night, but she quickly squelched the impulse. She desired to conduct herself as a lady, not a simpering water pot, she reminded herself sternly, her mouth firming as she stood her ground.

"As I do not have my companion with me, your lordship, I believe it would be best if I left the door slightly open," she said, pleased with the cool note in her voice. "I would not wish to give the locals any more to gossip about."

He raised a slashing eyebrow as if in amusement. "Are you afraid I may harm you?" he asked, his deep voice mocking. "If I may remind you,

Miss Haverall, 'tis you who assaulted me, and without provocation, I might add."

She flushed at his taunting words, her decision to act the proper lady forgotten. "There are some who would consider pushing one's way into a lady's bedchamber sufficient provocation to warrant a bullet!" she retorted, deciding the odious creature wasn't worthy of her efforts. "How did I know you weren't a criminal? You certainly don't look like any earl I've ever seen!" She added this last with a defiant toss of her head.

The earl's mouth lost its easy smile. "So I have been told," he said, his jade-green eyes meeting hers in a frosty stare. "But make no mistake, ma'am, I *am* an earl, and it is a crime to attack a member of the House of Lords. Would you care to know the punishment?"

Portia fought back her fear, determined not to show this menacing bully the slightest weakness. "I am aware of the punishment, my lord."

"It is transportation to a penal colony," he continued as if she hadn't spoken. "And do not think your sex will protect you. I am acquainted with the magistrate hereabouts, and he does not hold with criminals, regardless of their gender."

"I am not a criminal!"

"Nor am I, and I do not appreciate being treated like one merely because I do not look as you think an earl should look. Now please shut the door and be seated. You have my word as a gentleman that I won't harm you."

Portia gave in with a frustrated sigh. "I was only trying to observe the proprieties," she muttered, missing the amusement in his eyes as she closed the door with a slam. "You must know it is unseemly for us to be alone without benefit of a chaperone."

"And do you always do what is seemly?" he asked, his expression enigmatic as he studied her.

"I have been trying, although heaven knows why I make the effort." Portia admitted, settling in the chair he indicated. "It doesn't seem to have done me the slightest bit of good."

"Indeed?"

At the drawled word Portia glanced up, frowning at the smile softening his harsh features. "It is of no moment, sir," she said, thinking he wasn't nearly so fearsome-looking when he smiled. "What is it you wished to discuss?"

"A great deal, actually." He took his seat, leaning back in his chair and crossed his feet in an indolent manner that made it plain he was in no hurry to end their conversation. "However, if it will soothe your sensibilities, my mother's maid will soon be joining us. She would be here now except I sent her to fetch us some tea."

"Your mother is with you?" Portia was surprised.

"Unfortunately not, else I would not find myself in this contretemps," he replied, his deep voice suddenly rueful. "She would never have allowed Miss Montgomery to give her the slip as I did. A rather determined lady, my mother. You would like her, I think."

"I am sure I would," Portia replied dutifully, wondering what his lordship was about. Before she could give the matter another thought the door opened and a plump maid came bustling in, a tray balanced in her large, competent hands.

"I've seen better food in a pig's trough, I have," she grumbled, setting the tray down in front of Portia. "Such stale bread and cakes as to make a beggar say, 'no, thank you.' I had to threaten the cook with me fists before she'd do a proper tea."

"Thank you, Gwynnen. We appreciate your herculean efforts." The earl took the maid's complaining chatter in stride. "Now kindly sit down and be quiet. I haven't finished talking to Miss Haverall as yet."

"You can talk while you're eating." The maid ignored him as she filled a plate with sandwiches and small cakes and handed it to Portia. "And you can listen and eat, Miss Haverall. Your maid says you but pecked at your breakfast."

Portia hid a quick smile, thinking Nancy had found a formidable ally in the earl's blunt maid. "Thank you," she said, accepting the plate with a gracious nod. "You are very kind."

It took several minutes before Gwynnen was satisfied with the amount of food on their plates and retired to a chair in the corner. The earl looked somewhat ill at ease trying to balance the cup and plate in his big hands, and Portia took malicious pleasure in his discomfort. He looked like a bear at a garden party, she thought, wondering how long it would be before he managed to crush the teacup he was handling so roughly.

"You said last night that you were related to the Countess of Lowton," he said without preamble, making Portia start with surprise. She looked up from her plate to find him studying her through narrowed green eyes.

"Yes, your lordship," she replied, bristling slightly at the implied doubt in his voice. "She is my great-aunt."

He eyed her with patent skepticism. "If that is so, perhaps you can explain your presence here. One would hardly expect a countess to allow an unmarried member of her family to put up at an inn when she must have several rooms available in her town house."

The mockery in his words caused Portia's hands to tighten about her cup. She longed to toss the dregs of her tea in his sneering face, but his taunt about the local magistrate made her cautious. She didn't truly believe he would have her taken up, but she thought it prudent not to press him too far.

"Apparently her ladyship did not receive the note informing her of my arrival," she said instead, shooting him a resentful glare. "She has gone to Scotland to visit her son, and as the staff is not well-acquainted with me, they could not permit me to stay. I have sent her a letter, however, and I am sure she will send for me once she knows I am here." She added this last somewhat defiantly.

If he noted her insolence he did not remark upon it. "And what of your family in . . . Where did you say you were from?" He took a lazy sip of tea, his eyes never leaving her face.

"Chipping Campden," she snapped, knowing full well she hadn't told him a single thing about herself.

He inclined his head in mocking politeness. "Chipping Campden, then. Would your family in Chipping Campden not worry about your staying at an inn? Surely they would prefer you return to them, rather than wait here for word from her ladyship."

Portia's face burned as she remembered her plans to use her father's death to soften his lordship's anger. "I have no family, my lord," she said, studying his face for any reaction. "My father died last year, and my mother passed on when I was but a girl. I have no siblings."

To her relief she saw a flicker of sympathy in his eyes as they rested briefly on the front of her gown. "I am sorry, Miss Haverall. I should have known by your dress that you are in mourning."

He added softly. "You have my condolences. I know it hurts to lose one's parent."

The compassion in his voice made Portia squirm with guilt. "May I ask why you are interested in my parents?" she queried, lowering her eyes to her cup as she struggled to control her errant emotions. She decided she preferred the earl's arrogance to his empathy. It was rather difficult deceiving someone who was being genuinely kind.

"It is not important." The earl's cool reply brought her head back up, and the hard look on his face made her swallow uneasily. "However, learning you are somewhat at loose ends does make things a great deal easier for me."

"What things?" Portia demanded, visions of herself dragged off to Australia in chains filling her head.

"Things such as your returning to York with me to act as my mother's companion." he said calmly, setting down his teacup and meeting her stunned look with a cool smile. "You have deprived me of one companion, Miss Haverall. Does it not seem only fair that you should be the one to replace her?"

3

Had he been in the mood, the incredulous expression on Miss Haverall's eloquent face would have made Connor chuckle with delight. She looked, he mused, like a child about to snatch a particularly choice sweet from the tray, only to have the nanny catch her in the act and rap her knuckles.

She blinked in obvious confusion. "I beg your pardon, my lord?"

He crossed his feet, and leaned back in his chair. "I wish you to act as my mother's companion," he repeated, relishing the heady sense of victory as he neatly closed the trap he had been laying since the moment she'd walked into the room. "She is an invalid, unable to travel, and she needs a young lady to bear her company. Miss Montgomery was to have served in that capacity, but thanks to your interference, she has escaped. Now Mother shall have to do without."

Miss Haverall set her cup down with a loud clatter. "Oh, for pity's sake!" she exclaimed, her brows meeting in an impatient scowl. "You make it sound as if the poor creature was your prisoner or some such thing! And for your information, sir, I did not 'interfere' in anything. Miss Montgomery came to *me*. I did not seek her out."

"Perhaps not." Connor conceded the point with

35

a cool nod. "But there is no denying that had you not . . . assisted her, shall we say, I would not now find myself without a companion for my mother. I love my mother, Miss Haverall, and I dislike intensely the thought that I may have failed her."

To his surprise she turned an alarming shade of white. "What do you mean?" she asked, her voice trembling slightly.

Her reaction made Connor frown. He'd meant to intimidate her, certainly, but not to terrorize her. He was painfully aware his appearance was frightening at the best of times, and he'd always gone out of his way never to use his size as a weapon. That he may have done so now shamed him, and he made a conscious effort to moderate his voice.

"I mean, Miss Haverall, that having traveled all the way from York to Cambridge to fetch Miss Montgomery, I have no intention of returning home empty-handed. I am asking that you and your maid come with me, and that you act as my mother's companion until I can arrange for a replacement."

She sat so quietly that he feared he'd offended her beyond all bearing. He cursed himself for listening to Gwynnen. Cursed himself some more for being so bloody blunt when he should have apologized for bursting into her room like a maddened rapist. No wonder she had hit him over the head, he thought, feeling lower than the vilest criminal. He sent her a tentative look before reaching out to take her hand.

"Is everything all right?" he asked, his tone gentle as he searched her misty gray eyes for some hint of what she was thinking. "I apologize if I have upset you. I assure you that was not my intention."

Portia gazed up at him, not knowing what to say. In the end she decided only the truth would suffice, and she drew a deep breath to steady herself. "I am not upset," she replied quietly, her heart racing as she met his brilliant green gaze. "It is just that I ... I know what it is to disappoint one's parent, and I quite sympathize with your plight."

"I see," Connor replied, feeling worse than before. Perhaps others were right to label him a beast, he decided morosely. Heaven knew he had done nothing but behave in the most beastlike manner since meeting Miss Haverall.

"Yes," Portia continued, "my father died last year, and prior to his death we quarreled incessantly. I know what a bitter disappointment I was to him, and as I told my maid, I do not blame him for disinheriting me."

Connor sat back, his eyes widening in disbelief. "He *disinherited* you?" he repeated, unable to believe that any father could treat his own child so shabbily.

Portia's face grew red with embarrassment. She hadn't meant to blurt that out, but having said it, there was little she could do but brazen it out. "Things aren't quite so grim as all that," she informed him with an uneasy laugh. "My mother left me well provided for, and I assure you I am far from destitute. Quite the opposite, in fact."

Connor said nothing, although he was far from convinced. Perhaps he should offer her the post permanently, he thought, and was about to do just that when she said, "Enough of me, my lord. I have been thinking, and I've decided to return to York and act as your mother's temporary companion. As you say, 'tis only fair."

"Then you agree you are at fault?" he asked, not certain what he should believe.

Her chin came up a fraction. "Not at all," she said coolly, defiance returning to her face. "This is all your doing from start to finish, but I see no reason why your mother should suffer merely because you have bungled things."

"*I* have bungled?" he repeated incredulously, his guilt vanishing under a wave of indignation.

She gave a brisk nod, apparently recovered from her earlier distress. "If you hadn't frightened Miss Montgomery she would never have fled to my room for sanctuary, and then I shouldn't have been obliged to knock you over the head with the bed warmer." Bluntly, she added, "Although I will grant you probably did not deliberately frighten Miss Montgomery. She struck me as being of a rather excitable disposition."

"Do you mean you do not think I meant to have my evil way with her?" he demanded in an aggrieved tone, wondering why he'd been so foolish as to think he had offended her. It was obvious the chit didn't have an ounce of propriety in her entire body.

Her eyes grew even frostier. "Had I thought that, my lord, I should have told you to go to the devil. Now, if you are quite finished with your attempts to put me to the blush, when would you like to leave?"

"I hope you know what we're about," Nancy grumbled, carefully folding a chemise and laying it in the portmanteau at her feet. "Your father would spin in his grave if he knew what you was doing."

Portia remembered one of her and her father's last quarrels and gave a bitter smile. "Nonsense, Nancy. Papa wouldn't be the slightest bit amazed by my actions," she said, hiding her pain with a light laugh. "Did I not threaten to run off and become a governess if he disinherited me?"

Nancy's eloquent snort let Portia know what she

thought of that bit of fustian. "Governesses is one thing; companions is another," she said, adding another chemise to the pile. "Well, at least that Gwynnen seems a sensible soul. She'll keep his lordship in his place, I don't doubt."

The memory of how the plump maid had bear-led her towering employer out of the room made Portia smile, despite her sad thoughts. "She did seem to have him nicely under the cat's paw," she said admiringly. "I wonder how she does it."

"Never you mind about that, Miss Portia," Nancy advised sharply. "You ought to be wondering how your great-aunt will react when she finds out you've gone dashing off to Yorkshire with the earl. That will take a fine bit of explaining, you mark my words."

Portia had already given the matter considerable thought. "Don't fret, Nancy. Aunt will be de-lighted to learn that the Countess of Doncaster, upon hearing of my sad plight, invited me to stay with her in her country home. How could she pos-sibly object?"

"She'll object plenty when she learns her lady-ship wasn't even here!" Nancy slammed the lid of the trunk closed and rose to her feet. "And if you think she won't find out, you're all about in your head! There will be more than enough folk eager to spill the truth to her."

"Perhaps, but Aunt will accept my version of events."

The cool certainty in Portia's voice made Nancy frown. "Why?"

Portia's lips curved in a cynical smile. "Because it is convenient for her to do so," she said sagely. "And if I have learned anything, it is that people will always believe what they *want* to believe. Truth has little to do with reality."

Nancy was silent for a long moment and then

shook her head. "I still don't understand why you are so set to go to York," she complained with a sigh. "I'd have thought that after last night, you'd never be wanting to clap eyes on his lordship again."

Portia wasn't sure how to respond. She lowered her eyes to the fichus in her lap, her fingers stroking the fine lace as she struggled to find the right words to make Nancy understand.

"Perhaps I see it as a way to make amends to Papa," she said, her shoulders lifting in an uneasy shrug. "I failed him so miserably, and I see no reason why the earl should have to fail his mother. Besides, it is only for a little while, and York is certain to be more agreeable than Chipping Campden." She added this with a light laugh, but it was obvious from the scowl on Nancy's face that her attempt at humor had fallen flat.

"Failed your father, indeed!" the maid muttered darkly, rolling up a stocking and adding it to the second portmanteau. "If you ask me, 'tis *he* who failed *you!* Cutting you out of his will only because you didn't want to wed that mutton-brained cousin of yours . . . ! Well—" She shook her head. "—far be it from me to speak ill of the dead, but I hope the old skinflint is properly sorry for what he has done!"

"But that was only money," Portia argued, sad she could not make Nancy see her point. "I failed him in a far more basic way, and I am determined to do whatever it takes to make amends. Now kindly finish the packing. His lordship wishes to leave as soon as possible."

They departed after a hasty luncheon, setting out for the north country in the earl's traveling coach. The carriage amused Portia, for it was as large and imposing as the earl himself. The body was painted a glistening black, and except for the gold and scarlet trim, it was completely free of adornments. The lack of a crest or other heraldic device surprised Portia. She would have thought a man so obviously aware of his rank as Doncaster would have announced the fact to the world.

Nancy and Gwynnen became instant friends, and while they were engaging in a comfortable gossip, Portia settled back to stare out the glazed window at the passing scenery. She would have preferred spending the time becoming better acquainted with the earl, but after muttering a curt "Good day" to her, he had buried his nose in a gazette. She was used to such behavior from her father, but for some reason Doncaster's indifference stung her pride. After all, she told herself peevishly, she was doing the dratted man a considerable favor. The very least he could do would be to acknowledge her existence!

She glanced away from the window to study him through narrowed eyes. His head was bent to the gazette, his attention fixed on whatever he was reading. If he wouldn't do her the courtesy of satisfying her understandable curiosity, she decided with a flash of her old mischievousness, then she would simply have to discern what she could on her own.

He was dressed for travel in a worn Garrick coat of gray wool, and the many-caped coat made him look even larger and more imposing than ever. Upon entering the coach he'd set his hat and gloves aside with an impatience that told her he seldom bothered with such items, an observation that was confirmed by his tanned and work-worn hands. As it had been this morning, his dark hair was pulled back in a queue. It was a style she associated with men of her father's generation, yet it looked oddly right on the earl. She bit her lip in amusement, a sudden vision of Doncaster, his hair arranged in a mass of curls *à la Byron*, springing to mind.

"Is there something I can do for you, Miss Haverall?" The earl's cold voice dissolved the image, and Portia looked up to find him watching her with his brilliant green eyes.

She flushed at being caught gaping at him like a schoolgirl. "I was wondering about your mother, my lord," she said, speaking coolly to hide her embarrassment. "I believe you said she is an invalid?"

His expression grew even more remote as he turned to gaze out the window. "She was injured in a fall from a horse last year, and is not yet able to walk." His clipped words made it obvious he still found the topic a painful one. "The doctors have no explanation for it, but then, they seldom do."

The suffering in his voice made Portia forgot her annoyance with him. "I am sorry, my lord."

"It was my fault," he continued, his hands clenching into fists. "We had guests, and they wished to go hunting. I've never seen the sense in chasing some poor, defenseless fox all about creation, and so I refused to accompany them. I thought that would be the end of it, but I hadn't reckoned with Mother's stern sense of duty. She took them out on her own and lost her seat going over a hedge."

Portia gave an involuntary gasp. One of her neighbor's sons, a young man in his twenties, had been killed in a similar accident. The countess had to be in her fifties at least, and the wonder was that she had survived the fall at all. Portia knew she should say something to that effect to the earl, but if the bitter look on his face was any indication, she doubted the words would bring him much comfort.

"That is why I am so determined you should act as her companion until I can hire a new one," Doncaster said, his gaze fastened once more on her face. "I put her in that Bath chair. The least I can do is see that she lacks for nothing."

Portia's heart dropped to her toes at the stark declaration. She'd wanted to become better acquainted with the earl, she reminded herself with a heavy sigh, and it would seem she had received her wish. Unsure what to say, she turned back to the window.

Connor watched her, angrily cursing himself when he saw the shock she was taking such pains to hide. A taciturn man by nature, he could hardly believe he had been so forthcoming with her. It was her eyes, he decided, shifting uncomfortably on his seat. They were direct and clear, and they looked at a man as if they could see clear to his soul.

Her dark-brown hair was pulled back from her face in an elegant chignon, but he had no trouble remembering how it had looked still tousled from sleep and streaming down her back. She was dressed in the first crack of fashion in a traveling ensemble of gray and maroon, and he had to admit she was a fetching sight. She was as delicate and lovely as a piece of Dresden china, and looking at her now, he found it hard to believe she was the same virago who had crowned him with a bed warmer.

The uncomfortable silence that had fallen between them continued as the carriage wound its way northward. Even Gwynnen and Nancy had stopped talking, and by the time they reached the inn where they would be taking their tea, Portia's nerves felt stretched to the breaking point. Her

head was pounding from the tension and the
swaying of the coach, and as she stepped down
from the carriage she would have stumbled had it
not been for the earl's hand at her elbow.

"Are you all right, Miss Haverall?" he asked, his
tone solicitous as he took in her pale features.
"Shall I carry you?"

The thought of being carried to the inn like a
silly female in a swoon was all it took to stiffen
Portia's spine. "I am quite all right, my lord," she
said, her tone firm as she gazed past his broad
shoulder. "My foot slipped on a rock, that is all."

He gave her a measured look but took a step
back, allowing her to continue on her own. They
were greeted at the door by the innkeeper, who escorted them into a private parlor where a fire was
blazing in the hearth. After stepping into the ves-
tibule to wash her hands and face, Portia hurried
forward to warm herself by the fire. She was enjoying her second cup of tea when the earl joined
her.

"We should reach Hawkshurst by evening." he
said, his eyes intent on her face. "Are you certain
you feel up to continuing? You are still quite pale."

His concern pleased Portia, even as it annoyed
her. She detested women who behaved as if every
ill wind would blow them away, and it irked her
that he should take her for such a puling creature.
On the other hand, she couldn't remember the last
time anyone had expressed such interest in her
well-being. It was oddly touching, and because
she liked the sensation so much, she pushed it
away with a scowl.

"I should have thought that last night would
have shown you that I am no milk-and-water
miss," she said, raising her chin until she was gazing straight into his startlingly green eyes. "A car-

riage journey is well within my poor powers, I assure you."

The belligerent tone in her voice as well as the defiant tilt to her chin had no discernible effect on the earl. "We will leave within the hour," he said, his voice as cold and smooth as ice. He then rose to his feet and left the room.

Portia watched him go, more than a little ashamed of her shrewish performance. So much for her vow to be a lady, she thought with an unhappy sigh. It was apparently going to prove far more difficult than she had anticipated.

It was approaching twilight as they arrived at the earl's estate, which was located some five miles from York. The manor house had been built during the middle part of the last century, and its elegant lines and graceful columns made the breath catch in Portia's throat. "It's beautiful," she whispered, her eyes filled with awe as she turned to Doncaster.

Connor gazed at the house, feeling the same sense of joy he always felt when returning home. "Yes, it is," he said, the quiet pride of ownership evident in his deep voice. "Shall we go inside? I am sure my mother will be waiting to meet you."

To Portia's disappointment, however, the countess had already retired for the evening, leaving a message that she would meet her new companion in the morning. Gwynnen paused long enough to explain that her ladyship often retired early, and then hurried upstairs to attend her mistress. Nancy also excused herself to see to the unpacking, and Connor and Portia were left to eye each other uncertainly. Connor was the first to break the uneasy silence.

"We normally take our meals at country hours, Miss Haverall," he said, clearly making a determined effort to be polite. "Would you care to join me for dinner in an hour?"

Portia hesitated, knowing the earl was extending the olive branch to her. The thought of food was tempting, but not so tempting as a hot bath and a soft bed. Although she knew she should accept, she shook her head with regret.

"If your lordship has no objections, I would rather have a tray in my room," she said, offering a soft smile of apology. "It has been rather a long day."

"Yes, it has," he agreed, so solemnly that Portia was uncertain whether he was relieved or disappointed. "In that case, ma'am, allow me to bid you good night. I shall be gone when you awaken, but after lunch I should be happy to show you about the place. Do you ride?"

She debated whether or not to own to the truth, then shrugged her shoulders in resignation. Her deficiency would be more than obvious to his lordship the first time she tried to take a fence. "After a fashion," she confessed with a self-deprecatory laugh. "We usually rented our hacks as we needed them, and the only chance I had to ride was when I visited my friends in the country. But I'm a fast learner," she added somewhat anxiously, lest he think her a complete ninnyhammer.

He studied her for a moment, and then his mouth curved in a smile that made her heart race. "Of that, Miss Haverall, I make no doubt," he drawled, his eyes bright with the first flash of warmth she'd seen in hours. "Until tomorrow, then."

The room to which the maid conducted her was the most luxurious Portia had ever seen. The walls were papered in a bright-yellow print that was vaguely Oriental, and the furniture was a charming collection of delicate Queen Anne and gilded Italian rococo. After indulging herself in a soak in the copper tub set before the fire, Portia climbed into the high, canopied bed to enjoy the tray of tea and cakes that had been delivered by a giggling parlor maid.

"It seems I've been deceived all these years," she remarked to Nancy, her expression rueful as she glanced about her. "The lot of a companion isn't nearly so grim as I have been led to believe. It's quite comfortable, in fact."

"Don't let this fool you, Miss Portia," the older woman warned sagely as she arranged Portia's brushes on the polished surface of the dressing table. "This is a guest room, not servant's quarters like you'd have in another house. Although," she added grudgingly, "even the servants' rooms here aren't so bad. I have my own room."

"You do?" Portia was impressed. At home Nancy had had to share her cramped room beneath the eaves with the other maid. "The house must be quite large, then."

"Thirty rooms, not counting the servants' quarters," Nancy provided, repeating what Gwynnen had told her. "And there's a town house in London, too, although it's not been used in years."

The tea and the delicious food, along with the warm bath, were beginning to have a soporific effect on Portia. She set the tray on the side table and snuggled down beneath the thick covers. "Really?" she asked around a yawn, her eyes already drifting closed. "Why is that?"

"Gwynnen didn't say, miss, but I think it's got something to do with the earl. Gwynnen said his lordship won't go to London, not even for Parliament."

"Mmm." Sleep beckoned, and Portia welcomed it gratefully. Her last conscious thought was to won-

der why a man so obviously duty-bound as
Doncaster should be so neglectful in his responsibil-
ities. She'd have to speak to him on the matter ...

"So you're the young lady who tried to kill my
son with a bed warmer." Lady Elizabeth Dewhurst's bright-green eyes, a color she had be-
queathed her son, sparkled with amusement as
she greeted Portia. "Well, I suppose I ought to be
grateful your aim wasn't any better. Come closer,
and let me have a look at you."

Portia bit back a smile as she obeyed the older
woman's teasing command. She'd walked into the
countess's bedchamber expecting to find a wan
and fading woman, but the vibrant lady dressed to
the nines in a fashionable gown of lilac silk was
the furthest thing from an invalid she had ever encountered. Indeed, had her ladyship not been sitting in a Bath chair, she would have suspected the
earl of spinning her a Banbury tale.

"Ah, that is better." Lady Eliza's lips curved in
a pleased smile as she studied Portia with un-
abashed curiosity. "Yes, you'll do nicely, I think.
What did you say your name was?"

"I am Miss Portia Haverall, my lady," Portia
said recognizing the earl's full mouth and high
cheekbones in his mother's face. "My great-aunt is
Lady Lowton. Do you know her?"

"Georgianne? I should say I do. But don't think
I shall hold that against you," the countess informed her with a tinkling laugh. "We are none of
us responsible for our relations, and I thank God
for it. My own family, I fear, leaves a great deal to
be desired. Whigs, you know."

"No, my lady, I did not," Portia answered,
thinking what a shame it was that the earl had not
inherited his mother's warmth and wit along with

her good looks. "I shall try to remember that, and not say anything insulting about the party."

"Oh, you may say what you like, for it can't be any worse than what Connor says. A Tory, like his father, for all the notice he takes of politics as a whole. Sheep, now—sheep are another matter, for he positively dotes on the tiresome creatures. Do you know anything about sheep?"

The leap in the discussion made Portia smile. "No, my lady, I fear I do not," she said, thinking she would enjoy the coming days with the countess. Perhaps she'd even tell his lordship there was no hurry in finding a new companion. Until she heard from her great-aunt, she had nowhere else to go.

The countess gave a dejected sigh. "Pity," she said, the jewels on her fingers winking as she threaded them together. "Ah, well, it was too much to hope, I suppose. Shall we have tea, then? I shall tell you about our home and you may tell me about yourself. I want to know all about the young lady who managed to get the best of my son."

Portia's first morning at Hawkshurst passed quite pleasantly. The countess was a delight, and by luncheon Portia felt as if she'd known the other woman all her life. Lady Eliza had a wry sense of humor, and she showed a lively interest in everything and everyone about her. Portia decided it was because her infirmity made it difficult to leave the house, and tried not to take offense when she began quizzing her about her wardrobe.

"I can understand why you would wish to continue mourning for your father," the countess remarked as Portia wheeled her Bath chair into the dining room. "But surely a bit of color would not be considered improper after all these months! A deep-sapphire, perhaps, or ruby-red. You would look lovely in red."

Portia recalled a gown she had seen in one of the gazettes. It had been fashioned of shimmering red silk, with tiny puff sleeves and a décolletage that was just this side of proper. It was precisely the sort of gown she would have favored in her old life, but now that she was determined to be a lady, she put the dress firmly from her mind.

"It is very kind of you to say so, my lady." she replied quietly, "but I am afraid such colors are unsuitable for an unmarried lady."

"Posh!" Lady Eliza retorted, shooting Portia a disbelieving look. "You can not mean that nonsense! However is an unmarried lady to attract a husband at all if she goes about draping herself in dismal grays?"

Portia was uncertain how to respond to the scorn in the countess's voice. Chipping Campden was a small village to be sure, but they had never lacked for assemblies and other entertainments. She'd had ample opportunities to observe how the *ton* conducted themselves, and one of the things she noted first was the importance they placed in appearance, a preoccupation she had always viewed with an amused sense of superiority.

"I did not mean to imply that I would dress as a sparrow, your ladyship," she said at last, choosing her words with care. "But neither do I intend to deck myself out as a peacock. I would not wished to be considered fast."

"Better to be thought fast than a slowtop," Lady Eliza retorted, her expression making it obvious she was far from pleased. She slumped lower in her chair, her fingers drumming an impatient staccato on the chair's front lever. Suddenly she straightened, her expression softening as she smiled at Portia.

"If it is a matter of money which is making you hesitate, I am sure Connor can be persuaded to advance you some funds on your salary," she suggested gently. "He mentioned your father had disinherited you, and if your purse is a bit light, I should be more than happy to help you."

Portia's cheeks flushed a bright-rose. "It is not the money, my lady," she muttered, all but writhing in embarrassment as she realized the countess thought her destitute. "My father may have cut me from his will, but I still receive a considerable sum from my mother. I am not quite an heiress, but so long as I am prudent, I shall never lack for anything."

"Now I have offended you," the countess said, looking properly penitent. "I didn't mean to. No one knows more than I what it is to have more pride than pounds in one's pocket, and I only wished to help. May I hope you will forgive me?" She cast Portia a hopeful look.

Portia relented, ashamed for having upset the older woman. "Of course I shall forgive you," she said with a gentle smile. "And now that you mention it, I suppose a few gowns would not go amiss. It seems forever since I have had anything new."

"And the colors?" the older woman asked, quick to press her advantage. "You *will* choose something bright and cheerful, won't you? I know you must think me an interfering old lady," she added when she saw Portia hesitate, "but I adore clothes, and it is no fun choosing gowns for myself so long as I am stuck in this thing." She indicated her Bath chair with a wave of her hand.

Portia leaned over and gave the countess's hand a gentle squeeze. "I will consider it," she promised, then settled back in her own chair and unfolded her napkin. They were just starting the soup course when she remembered the earl's promise to show her about the estate.

"Will his lordship be joining us for luncheon?" she asked, glancing out the large mullioned windows to the rolling hills of deep-green.

The countess gave a haughty sniff. "I am sure I do not know," she said, raising her spoon to her lips. "I am only his mama, and he seldom sees fit to inform me of his plans. Why do you ask?"

Before Portia could explain, the door to the dining room swung open, and Lord Doncaster strode in, dressed in clothing better suited to a laborer than a peer. "I am sorry I am late, Mother, Miss Haverall," he apologized, bending to press a kiss on his mother's delicate cheek. "There was trouble with seepage in the north field, and we have spent all morning trying to drain it."

The countess eyed her son's mud-spattered boots with pained resignation. "Talk to Mr. Willowby," she suggested before turning her attention back to her food. "Your father always set great store by that wily old shepherd."

"I'd forgotten he was back at the home farm," Connor said, his expression thoughtful as he took his seat. "Perhaps after luncheon I'll—"

"After luncheon you will take our guest for a ride," Lady Eliza interrupted, fixing Connor with a stern look. "Have Grayson consult with Mr. Willowby. The lad does little enough to warrant the salary you pay him."

"Mother—"

"Not that I blame Grayson, mind." Lady Eliza addressed her remarks to Portia. "The lad is quite good, but this son of mine refuses to give him any real responsibility. He considers it his duty to see to every little detail of the estate."

Portia saw the look of chagrined exasperation that flashed across the earl's face. It was obvious his mother kept him firmly under the cat's paw, and given her experiences with her father, she felt a surprising empathy for him.

"If your lordship is too busy to accompany me, I understand," she offered, not wishing to add to his discomfiture. "There will be other days, I am sure."

Rather than appreciating her charitable offer, he shot her an angry glare. "As I had already planned to take you about, Miss Haverall, there is no need to wait." His voice was as cool and remote as she remembered. "Shall we say twenty minutes after we have finished our meal?"

"Twenty minutes will be fine, sir," Portia responded stiffly, vowing it would be a cold day before she gave in to another altruistic impulse. It was just as she had always suspected: being a lady was a thankless task.

4

After luncheon Connor retired to his study for a quick look at his accounts while Miss Haverall went up to her rooms to change. He was going over his tenants' accounts when his mother, pushed by a footman, maneuvered her Bath chair through the door.

"Aha, I knew I'd find you here," she accused, bending a disapproving frown on him. "I thought you were taking Miss Haverall riding. What do you mean by holing up in here like a hermit?"

"I am but waiting for Miss Haverall to join me, ma'am, and then we will ride out," Connor replied, experiencing the familiar pang of shame he always felt when he saw his mother in the chair. Each time he remembered he was the one who put her there, the guilt would lay heavy on his heart.

"She is a lively thing," the countess said after dismissing the footman with a wave of her hand. "A trifle nice in her notions, perhaps, but I must say I like her much better than any of the others. Thank you for bringing her to me."

Connor left the papers on his desk and crossed the room to kneel beside her chair. "You know this is only temporary," he warned, hating the feeling that he was snatching away her happiness. "The moment I find you a new companion, Miss Haverall will join her great-aunt in Edinburgh."

"Yes, but that could take weeks," Lady Eliza reminded him, her lips curving in a crafty smile. "And even if you do hire some other silly girl, I do not see why I should lose Miss Haverall's company. She could always remain as our guest, could she not?"

Connor frowned as he considered his mother's suggestion. He'd already forgiven Miss Haverall for assaulting him with the bed warmer, but that didn't mean he was ready to welcome her as a permanent fixture in his home. "That is so," he conceded with a sigh, "but I think we should wait before suggesting it to her. She may have other plans, or her great-aunt may not grant her permission to remain."

"Posh." Lady Eliza dismissed his objections with another wave of her hand. "I am sure Georgianne will be delighted to have the child remain with us. Now, where do you mean to take our guest?"

"I thought to show her the north fields near the old Roman ruins," Connor replied, accepting the change of subject with resignation. It was a familiar ploy of his mother's, and he knew better than to argue with her.

"Excellent." Lady Eliza nodded her approval of the plan. "Although we spoke only briefly I gather she is something of a bluestocking, and I am sure she will enjoy seeing something so ancient. Perhaps you might translate some of the carvings for her. You took honors in Latin when at school." She added this last with a spark of maternal pride that made Connor smile.

His classical studies had been the favorite part of his years at Oxford, and he'd enjoyed losing himself in his books. If only the rest of his time there had passed half so pleasantly, he thought, his eyes growing bitter as he remembered the humiliation he had suffered out of the classroom.

A sound at the door drew him away from his dark thoughts, and he glanced up as Miss Haverall hurried into the room.

"I am sorry if I kept you waiting, my lord," Portia apologized, feeling flushed and rushed after having spent the past half hour attempting to pin up her old riding habit. She'd lost a great deal of weight in the fifteen months since buying the habit, and it had taken all of Nancy's skills to make it fit with some semblance of style.

"Not at all, Miss Haverall," Connor replied, his deep voice giving no indication of the pleasure her appearance gave him. Her habit was fashioned of mulberry serge, lavishly trimmed with gold and black braid, and it showed her delicate figure to advantage. A velvet hat of the same color with a black veil and curving feather completed the ensemble, and he thought she looked completely enchanting.

"What a charming habit, my dear!" Lady Eliza exclaimed, clasping her hands together. "There, did I not tell you bright colors would suit you?"

"Yes, my lady." Portia's cheeks grew warm at the countess's praise and the admiration in the earl's eyes. "I know it's not appropriate for mourning, but—"

"Nonsense," Lady Eliza interrupted, her tone indicating she would brook no opposition. "It is perfectly lovely, and as it is doubtful you and Doncaster will encounter anything other than sheep on your ride, I am sure it hardly signifies. Off with you now." She gave them both a stern look. "And I don't want you to bring her back, Connor, until she has roses in her cheeks. She is much too wan."

* * *

Half an hour later Connor and Portia were riding over the green hills, the cool, damp wind stinging their faces. When they reached the top of a rise, Portia pulled up on her horse's reins and turned to the earl with a laugh of sheer delight.

"I hope your mother will be satisfied with the roses in my cheeks, my lord," she teased, forgetting her reserve in the pleasure of the moment. "My face feels as if it is frozen!"

Connor leaned forward in the saddle, the reins held competently in his hands as his gaze rested on her flushed features. "Do you wish to turn back?" he asked, determined to act the dutiful host.

"Heavens, no!" she exclaimed with a light laugh, her eyes dancing. "I was only funning, my lord, I assure you. Do let us go on."

An emotion he refused to identify as relief welled in Connor's heart, and he inclined his head in a grave manner. "There are some ruins just over the next hill," he said, indicating the direction with his riding crop. "They are said to be Roman in origin, although I have my doubts."

"That sounds delightful, sir," Portia replied, remembering the many ruins she'd seen in the area around Colchester when on holiday with her father. She'd been captivated at the thought of standing in the same spot where eighteen hundred years ago the emperor Claudius had stood, and she'd enthusiastically thrown herself into researching every detail she could find of the Romans. She smiled sadly, recalling how she and Papa had disagreed over the influence of Roman architecture on the Normans. He'd cut her out of his will for almost two months before finally restoring her.

Less than ten minutes later, she and the earl were standing before massive columns of marble

that had been stained black from centuries of
grime. She ran her gloved hands over the grooves
cut deep in the ancient stone, awed at their im-
mense size and age. "Why do you doubt that they
are Roman?" she asked, slanting him a curious
look. "They look much like the other ruins I have
seen. And that is Latin." She pointed at the words
carved above the arch.

"Yes, but a Latin of a much later period than the
Roman occupation," he answered, enjoying her in-
quisitiveness. The last time he'd showed the ruins
to a lady she'd pronounced them frightful and
asked to be taken home. Or perhaps it was himself
the lady had found frightful, he thought, remembering that the lady had departed Hawkshurst
soon afterward.

"I had no idea there was any difference between
one form of Latin or another," Portia said, apparently much struck by the thought. "Why would it
change?"

"All language changes," he replied, stepping
closer to indicate a specific word. "Do you see
that? *Dei*. It is Latin for 'God.' The Romans prac-
ticed polytheism, the worship of more than one
god, and has this been one of their buildings, they
would have dedicated it to a specific god like Ju-
piter or Minerva. I would say this was probably a
chapel or a monastery, and that it dates from a
later period, possibly the twelfth or thirteenth century."

"Indeed?" The casual expertise he displayed intrigued Portia, and she tilted her had to one side
to give him a considering look. "You seem certain
in your facts, sir. Is antiquities an interest of
yours?"

Connor hesitated, as if unwilling to share so private a part of himself. "You might say that," he
said at last, his eyes fixed on the ruins. "I made a

study of it while at Oxford." He turned his head suddenly, his eyes narrowing at the expression on her face. "Why are you smiling?"

Portia gave a guilty start at being caught behaving so poorly. "No reason, my lord," she denied, and then spoiled her disavowal by adding, "It is just that you do not look like a scholar, and I find it difficult imagining you bent over a pile of dusty books."

"I see," Connor answered, his lips twitching at her disarming frankness. "And pray, what does a scholar look like, Miss Haverall?"

"Slender, interestingly pale, with shabby clothes and a vague, distracted air about him."

He blinked at her prompt reply. "That is certainly specific enough," he said, leaning one broad shoulder against the pillar as he studied her. "Might I ask how you came to be so familiar with the species? Have you an older brother?"

"Not at all, but my father was a literature don at Cambridge, and he always had a half dozen or so of the creatures trailing after him." Portia's expression softened as she recalled those halcyon days of her childhood when their house had been filled with the sound of male voices raised in earnest argument. She used to sit on the steps in her night rail, listening entranced as her father discussed Shakespeare and Milton with his students until the wee hours of the morning.

There was nothing he had liked more than a good debate, and he always favored those students who dared to disagree with him. Perhaps that was why she had begun defying him, she mused with a sudden flash of insight. She hadn't been purposefully obtuse, as he had so often accused. She'd been trying to win his approval.

Connor was watching her closely, as if trying to read her thoughts. "Shall we start back, Miss

Haverall?" he asked, pushing himself away from
the pillar to stand over her. "The wind is rather
sharp today, and I wouldn't wish you to become
chilled."

Portia nodded distractedly, still lost in her troubling thoughts. He helped her remount, easily lifting her onto the saddle. They rode back a different
way, and Portia emerged from her bleak memories
long enough to notice her surroundings. They
were riding past a clear brook tumbling and froth-
ing over sharp, black stones, and she pulled her
horse to a halt to admire it.

"How beautiful," she said, sighing as she listened to the musical sound of rushing water. "I've
always thought of Yorkshire as a cold, desolate
place, but this is lovely."

Connor leaned forward in his saddle. "It is
that," he said, his voice filling with pleasure and
satisfaction as he gazed out at his land. "But don't
let the beauty of this place blind you to its true nature," he warned, his eyes coming to rest on her
features. "It may appear civilized, but beneath the
surface it is wild and dangerous. You would do
well to remember that."

Portia nodded silently, thinking the description
could also be applied to the earl himself. Except in
his case the wild danger was all too obvious, she
decided, stealing a thoughtful glance at him as
they resumed their ride.

Dressed as he was now, in a plain jacket of black
wool, his white stock tied carelessly about his
tanned throat, and his dark hair pulled back from
the sharp planes of his face, he looked utterly at
home in the harsh surroundings. She remembered
how out of place he had seemed in the inn's
shabby parlor, and realized this was his true ele-
ment. For all his fine title and great wealth, he was
really a simple farmer, and she found she admired

him the more for it. The realization kept her quiet
for the remainder of their ride.

Within a week of her arrival Portia felt as if
she'd been at Hawkshurst forever. She and the
countess had become fast friends, and Portia enjoyed every moment spent in the older woman's
company. Unlike most of the invalids she'd had
the misfortune of meeting, Lady Eliza didn't dwell
on her infirmities, but instead remained surprisingly cheerful. Not that she was all sweetness and
light, however. Lady Eliza was sharp-witted and
often sharp-tongued, and she kept Portia entertained with her wry observations of those about
her.

The countess also manipulated her brooding son
with a cunning combination of helplessness and
hectoring that left Portia wide-eyed with admiration. She'd come to regard her own tendency to
control those about her as unfeminine and unlady-
like, but no one could accuse the countess of being
anything other than a complete lady, and yet she
exercised complete command over her household.
For someone who had vowed to become a true
lady regardless of the cost, as Portia had, it was a
most illuminating observation.

Although her mornings were devoted to the
countess, her afternoons were her own. While
Lady Eliza slept, Portia either read or explored the
huge, elegant house. She was in the library one afternoon when the earl came upon her studying the
portraits of his ancestors.

"A smug-looking lot, are they not?" he drawled,
smiling as he gazed up at a painting of a dark-
haired man in velvet and lace. "Lord of all they
survey."

"Lord of this place, certainly," Portia answered,
her gaze shifting from the features painted on can-

vas to the man standing beside her. He had just come in from the fields, and he carried the smell of sweet hay and horses on him. That she should notice such a personal thing unnerved her, and she turned back to the portraits to cover her confusion.

"And who might this gentleman be?" she asked, her voice determinedly light. "He is certainly a fierce-looking fellow."

He glanced up at the portrait she indicated. "That is my grandfather, the fourth Earl of Doncaster."

Portia studied the man's dark hair and cold, remote expression. "You favor him," she said, recalling the first time she had seen him looming in her doorway.

The earl lifted his eyebrow as he gazed down at her. "Do I?" he asked, his deep voice edged with laughter. "That is hardly a compliment, you know. He was known as the Black Beast of Hawkshurst Hall, as much for his temper as his dark hair and eyes. I am said to resemble him in that as well."

The dryness in his tone told Portia he was teasing her, and she responded in kind. "Yes, I have noticed how the household quakes in fear of your fierce temper," she murmured, recalling how only that morning Gwynnen had scolded him soundly for tracking mud into his mother's sitting room.

Another portrait, that of a young lady with golden hair and wide blue eyes, caught her attention, and she moved closer to inspect it. "Who is this?" she demanded, caught by the sweetness of the woman's expression. "She is lovely."

An indulgent smile softened the edges of the earl's mouth. "That is my grandmother, the lady who tamed the Beast," he explained, his voice filled with obvious affection. "She died when I was a child, and I have few memories of her. I remember her playing the pianoforte. I believe she was quite talented."

A sudden memory of her own mother sitting at a pianoforte and picking out a tune flashed into Portia's mind. "My mother played the piano as well," she said, aware of the wistful note that had crept into her voice. "But I can't recall that she did so with any marked degree of ability." She shook off her sadness, and flashed him an impish smile. "In that, my lord, I am said to resemble her."

His green eyes sparkled in understanding. "Do you mean to say you are not a gifted musician, Miss Haverall?" he challenged. "You disappoint me. I thought all proper young ladies excelled at music and watercolors."

Portia's enjoyment with the situation vanished, and she glanced back at the portrait. "A proper young lady, your lordship, would never dream of excelling at anything," she said with a forced laugh. "To do so might lead to her being labeled intelligent, or, even worse, intellectual, and you must know that would never do."

"Why not?" He was frowning at the sharpness in her voice that her laughter couldn't quite disguise. "Better to be considered clever than foolish, I should think."

"Ah, that is because you are a man, sir," she said, her tone bitter. "A man is supposed to have a brain, and he is granted leave to use it freely. But for a woman to do likewise is considered an impropriety of the worse sort. Men will shake their heads at her and call her a bluestocking, a sobriquet certain to destroy any young lady's hope of achieving a match."

The earl's expression grew hard, and he drew

himself up to his full height. "I think you are being rather harsh in your assessment of the male of the species, Miss Haverall," he said coolly. "Men are not the only ones who unfairly label others. Your sex is also guilty of passing judgment and affixing cruel names to innocent men."

Given the many times she had suffered the cutting tongues of some of her neighbors's brattish daughters, there was no honest way Portia could deny his icy observation, but that didn't mean she was willing to concede the field to him. Instead she turned to face him, her chin tilted at a defiant angle.

"That may be, my lord," she said, her cheeks flushed with temper, "but it isn't often a gentleman so labeled would find himself on the shelf. Indeed, from what I have observed there's nothing a man likes more than to have an amusing name affixed to him. It is rather like a reputation, I suppose: desirable in a man, fatal in a woman."

The earl's jaw clenched in anger, and his eyes became as frosty as a winter's morning. "If you believe that, Miss Haverall, then you are an even bigger widgeon than I suspected," he said, his tone as icy as his eyes. "Now if you will pardon me, I must go and change. Good day to you." And he strode off, leaving Portia glaring after him.

Three days after her confrontation with the earl, Portia was sitting in the countess's study, a pile of letters heaped on the desk in front of her. Her ladyship maintained a correspondence with what appeared to be half the *ton*, and one of Portia's most important duties was to help her sort through the letters that arrived with each day's post. She had just handed one missive to the countess and was in the process of opening another when she heard the older woman give a heavy sigh.

"Is something amiss, my lady?" Portia asked, the open letter held loosely in her hand as she glanced up. "You haven't had bad news, I trust?"

"No, no, good news, in fact," Lady Eliza replied, setting the letter to one side with another sigh. "My neighbor and dear friend, Lady Alterwaithe, is returning home next week, and she has written asking permission to call on me."

"I see," Portia answered, uncertain if she should press for further explanation. "Would you like me to write a letter of regret to her ladyship?" she asked, decided that must be what was distressing the other woman.

"What?" Lady Eliza looked briefly mystified, then shook her head. "Oh, no, not at all," she said, lifting the cup of tea she had been drinking and studying its contents. "I am looking forward to seeing dearest Henrietta again. It is just . . . " Her voice trailed off.

"It is just what, my lady?" Portia prompted gently.

"It is just that she writes that her niece and a friend are returning with her, and she wishes to introduce them to me."

"Yes?" Portia could sense no great catastrophe in so mundane a request.

"Don't you see?" Lady Eliza exclaimed, setting her cup aside with a clatter. "It's not *me* Henrietta wishes them to meet, it is Connor, and you must see that that is quite impossible!"

"But why?" Portia demanded, more puzzled than ever. "I should think you would be grateful your friend wishes to introduce his lordship to two eligible young ladies! There can't be many marriageable females in this part of Yorkshire."

"But that's precisely my point!" Lady Eliza

wailed, wringing her hands in agitation. "There isn't but a handful of young ladies of rank left in the entire neighborhood who don't swoon at the very mention of my son's name, and now Henrietta means to bring two of them to tea! If Connor succeeds in frightening them off as well, whatever will become of him? He will die a bachelor, and the line along with him!"

The older woman's distress left Portia speechless. Until this moment it had never occurred to her that unmarried males suffered the same harping from anxious parents as did unmarried females. The realization struck her as highly diverting, but as it was obvious the countess did not consider the matter one for levity, she wisely kept her amusement to herself.

"I can see your ladyship's concern," she replied carefully, striving to keep her tone even. "But if the earl doesn't meet any ladies, will he not suffer the same fate regardless?"

"Eventually, I suppose," Lady Eliza conceded, looking so unhappy that Portia's heart went out to her. "But I was hoping with time I could make him more acceptable. You must agree that no lady in her right mind would take him as he is now."

"My lady!" Portia stared at the countess in astonishment. The older lady's sharp words reminded her of that last bitter argument with her father, and it hurt her that the woman of whom she had grown so fond could pass such a harsh assessment of her son.

Lady Eliza flushed guiltily at Portia's stunned expression. "Now you are thinking that I must be the most unnatural mother alive," she said, her eyes misting with tears, "and I suppose you are right. It is just that I worry about Connor. I want him happy, I want him married, and that will never happen so long as he persists in behaving so churlishly."

The countess's tears as well as the anxiety in her voice made Portia relax. Still, she felt oddly obliged to defend the earl, despite that she was somewhat hipped with him. "I haven't observed his lordship to behave with any marked degree of impropriety," she lied, her eyes not quite meeting Lady Eliza's.

The older woman refused to be taken in by such sophistry. "You hit him over the head with a bed warmer within seconds of clapping eyes on him," she reminded Portia with a sniff. "Laid him quite out, according to Gwynnen."

Portia's cheeks flamed with color. "He had just forced his way into my room!" she exclaimed, eyes sparkling with indignation. "What else was I to do?"

"Oh, I am not condemning you for your actions." Lady Eliza dismissed her protest with a wave of her hand. "I agree you behaved as well as any lady might under similar circumstances. But again, you miss my point." She leaned forward, her gaze earnest as she captured Portia's hand in hers.

"Connor had no right to force his way into your room," she said in a stern voice, "and it is precisely that penchant for brutish conduct that renders him so ineligible as a *parti*. How do you think a delicately bred young lady would respond to such provocation, hmm? She'd faint dead away, and any hopes I had of getting him married off would vanish like so much smoke."

"Perhaps," Portia agreed, reluctantly remembering Miss Montgomery's reaction to the earl. "But I still say you are refining too much on the matter. Besides, what can you do about it? The earl is a grown man, and he is hardly likely to change his behavior at this late date."

Lady Eliza beamed at her in delight. "Exactly so, my dear, and that is why we—you and I—must change it for him."

5

Lord, he was exhausted, Connor thought, brushing the sweat-dampened hair from his forehead as he wearily climbed the front steps leading to the house. It had been a hellish day, filled with frustrating, backbreaking work, and he wanted nothing more than to bolt down his supper and crawl into bed. He was contemplating forgoing the food entirely when the door opened and his butler greeted him with a bow.

Connor stopped in mid-step, his brows gathering in a frown as he studied his majordomo. Williams had been with him only a short while, but Connor knew the older man thought entirely too much of his own consequence to answer the door like a common footman. That he had deigned to do so boded ill, and Connor straightened his shoulders with a reigned sigh. "What is it, Williams?" he asked heavily, saying a mental goodbye to his hopes for a quiet evening.

"Her ladyship and Miss Haverall are waiting for you in the drawing room, my lord," Williams replied, his face expressionless as he took in his master's disheveled appearance. "They ask that you join them there."

Connor bit back an oath. "Now?" he demanded, making no effort to hide his displeasure.

Williams paused, a bushy eyebrow arching as he

gave Connor a cool look. "I am sure her ladyship will understand if you wish to change first," he said with an eloquent sniff. "Shall I inform her you will be with her shortly?"

Connor glanced down at his dusty jacket and grass-stained breeches, realizing he was in no fit state to grace anything other than a stable. He opened his mouth to agree, then abruptly closed it again. The devil take it, he thought sourly, his lips thinning with impatience. If his mama and Miss Haverall were so anxious to see him, then he would be happy to oblige them. He raised his eyes to meet his butler's disapproving gaze. "The drawing room, did you say?"

"Yes, my lord." William's features unfroze enough to acquire an anxious mien. "However, I feel you should—" He broke off in resignation as the earl turned and stalked away.

The door to the drawing room was closed, and Connor pushed it open with an angry shove, his jaw set as he prepared to do battle. His mother and Miss Haverall were sitting beside a blazing fire, and he greeted them both with a cool nod.

"You wished to see me, ma'am?" he asked, making no move to join them.

If she noted the sullen note in his voice, his mother gave no indication. Instead she beamed at him with undisguised pleasure, holding out her arms in welcome. "Ah, Connor, there you are!" she exclaimed happily. "Stop hovering in the doorway and come greet your mama properly. I have not seen you in days!"

Connor pushed himself away from the door, feeling a stab of guilt at his boorish behavior. He crossed the room, his annoyance forgotten as he bent to press a kiss on her cheek. "You saw me yesterday at dinner," he reminded her, smiling as he drew back to study her face. He thought she

looked less pale than she had of late, and the realization pleased him.

"Yes, *saw* you was about all I did," Lady Eliza
returned with a pretty pout. "You scarce said more
than a dozen words, and you left before the dessert was served. Had it not been for dear Portia, I
should have been left to converse with the
sylabub!"

The image of his mother talking earnestly to a
dessert glass of meringue and wine brought a
twinkle to Connor's eyes. "My apologies, Mama,
but as I told you Lady Gold was in foal, and—"

"Yes, yes, I know," she interrupted, waving
aside his apologies with a graceful hand. "And I
wasn't scolding you . . . precisely. Was I, dearest?"
She turned to her companion for confirmation of
her good intentions.

"Indeed you were not, my lady," Miss Haverall
assured her. "You were the very model of re-
straint."

"There? You see?" His mother gave him a trium-
phant smile and patted the settee beside her.
"Now sit down and tell us how you have spent
your day. You've been with the cows, if your
clothing is any indication."

Before answering, Connor accepted the cup of
tea and plate of delicacies Miss Haverall handed
him. "We moved the herd to the north pasture,"
he began, uncertain what details of his hectic day
would be suitable for a lady's ears. "Now that all
the calves have been delivered, it is time we began
fattening them for market. If prices hold, we'll
make a tidy profit by autumn."

"How wonderful!" His mother's face fairly radi-
ated maternal pride as she turned to Miss
Haverall. "Did I not tell you my son was brilliant?" she demanded, her smug tones making

Connor feel decidedly uncomfortable. "He knows exactly what he is about."

"He does seem quite competent," Miss Haverall agreed, turning to give him a commiserating smile. "What will your lordship do once the animals and crops have all been tended to?" she asked with every indication of interest. "Will you go to London?"

Connor grimaced at the mere notion. "Lord, no," he muttered, recalling his last visit to the teeming metropolis. "The only reason any sane man would wish to visit that pestilent place would be to attend Parliament, and as the present session will be ending next week, I see no reason why I should bother. Besides," he added as the thought suddenly struck him, "with the Season ending everyone will have returned home to the country."

His mother and Miss Haverall exchanged looks, and his mother picked up her teacup. "How interesting you should mention that," she began in a bright tone that made Connor immediately wary. "You'll never guess who has written me . . . Henrietta!"

"Henrietta who?" he prevaricated, wondering what his devious mama was up to this time.

"Now, Connor, don't be obtuse." She gave him a reproving frown. "You know perfectly well I am referring to my dear friend Lady Alterwaithe."

"Ah, yes," He managed not to shudder at the thought of his hen-witted neighbor. "How is the marchioness these days?"

"As well as can be expected, considering her advanced years," his mother answered, conveniently forgetting Lady Alterwaithe was but three years her senior. "She arrives home next week, and I thought it would be nice to have her over for tea. With your permission, of course."

"Mother—" Connor set his cup to one side, and reached out to cover her hand with his own "—you must know you may invite anyone you please. This is *your* home, after all."

"Of course I know that, dearest," Lady Eliza said, returning the pressure of his hand, "but I also know the last time I had guests you were so cool to them that they left highly insulted. Henrietta is one of my oldest friends, and I don't wish to subject either her or her guests to similar treatment. I should prefer having you admit outright that you've no use for company, rather than risk offending a caller. That is why I wished to have your permission before inviting anyone to tea."

Connor felt his face flush with color at the gentle rebuke. He remembered the incident only too well, and it was not precisely as his mother said. He'd gone out of his way to be pleasant to the young ladies who had descended upon them, but rather than being pleased with his attentions, they had acted as if he'd meant to ravish them on the spot. Indeed, one of them had actually swooned when he dutifully offered to show her his mother's prized orangery.

The unpleasant episode was the final straw that convinced him he was anathema to the fairer sex, and the thought of enduring another such experience was almost more than he could bear. It was on the tip of his tongue to ask her to refrain from issuing any further invitations, but at the hopeful look on her face he relented. What sort of son would he be to deny his mother the one source of pleasure she had in the world? he asked himself bleakly.

"Invite whomever you like, Mama," he said softly, carrying her hand to his lips. "I promise I shall be the soul of charm and courtesy to your guests. All right?"

His mother lowered her eyelashes, the edges of her mouth curving in a smile. "Very well," she said meekly, withdrawing her hand from his. "If you are certain you do not mind."

"Not at all," he lied, resolved. "In fact, I rather relish the thought of guests, and I am sure Miss Haverall would welcome company." He cast his mother's companion a polite look, and was puzzled by the bemused expression on her face.

"Company is always a welcome diversion, your lordship," she said, her eyes dancing despite her prosaic tones.

"Well, now that that is settled, I believe I shall go right up to my rooms and write dearest Henrietta at once!" His mother clapped her hands together like an eager child. "Portia, would you be so good as to ring for the footman for me?"

"Certainly, my lady." Miss Haverall's actions matched her words. "Would you like me to accompany you?" she asked as they waited for the footman to appear.

His mother gave a nervous start. "Heavens, no!" she exclaimed with a bright laugh. "You must know I can not compose so much as a single word with someone hovering about me. You may remain here with his lordship. I am sure the two of you must have a great deal to discuss with each other."

Connor slid Miss Haverall a considering look, noting that she seemed surprisingly unperturbed at the prospect of being left alone with him. The unmarried females he knew were seldom granted such a shocking degree of freedom, and he wondered that she did not insist upon accompanying his mother when she left. Perhaps she thought her age and dubious position gave her greater latitude, he mused, his brows gathering in a thoughtful frown. It also struck him as suspicious that his mama, usually a dragon of propriety, would even consider leaving them unchaperoned. His eyes gleamed as he contemplated the possible explanations.

They continued chatting until John, the sturdy footman who'd been hired to carry her ladyship about when she was not in her chair, arrived to take her upstairs. Miss Haverall made one final offer to attend his mother, but she refused even to hear of it. The moment the door was closed Connor turned to Miss Haverall.

"Subtlety was never Mama's forte," he drawled, slanting her a teasing grin. "I hope you do not mind?"

Portia returned the smile, relieved he had seen through his mother's ruse and wasn't offended. She couldn't abide humorless people, and she would have been disappointed with the earl had he been hipped. "Not at all, sir," she replied, inclining her head graciously. "I only hope that *you* are not offended. As you say, her ladyship was rather obvious in her desire to leave us alone."

"Yes," he agreed, "and as Mama is usually a stickler about such matters I can only conclude she is up to something devious." His gaze met hers in unmistakable challenge. "Have you any idea what that something might be?"

Portia set her teacup aside, accepting the challenge with alacrity. "As a matter of fact, I believe I do," she said. "Lady Eliza is looking forward to Lady Alterwaithe's visit, but she feels the prospect of company is not to your liking. Is that true?"

Connor was taken aback by the cool demand. "What nonsense," he retorted, scowling as he glance away. "You heard what I said to my mother, Miss Haverall. I have no objections to visitors. She may invite whomever she pleases."

"Having no objections is hardly a glowing testa-

ment, my lord," Portia said, trying not to wince
with guilt as she delivered the speech she and the
countess had spent the afternoon rehearsing.
"Your mother is afraid you'll be miserable with
the house filled with guests, and she is willing to
sacrifice her happiness to guarantee your own."

"But that is ridiculous!" Connor protested,
clearly appalled at the news. "I have told her a
dozen times that I . . ." His voice trailed off and he
gave her a suspicious look. "House filled with
guests?" he repeated. "I thought we were talking
about having Lady Alterwaithe over for tea."

"And so we were," she answered with a nod.
"But your mother was saying she was longing to
see her old friends again. Since she is no longer
able to travel, it makes more sense for them to
come to her, do you not agree?"

Connor rose to his feet to restlessly pace the
room. "Of course I agree," he said with a heavy
sigh, thrusting a hand through his dark hair. "It is
just . . ."

"Just what, my lord?" Portia pressed when he
did not continue.

Connor paused in front of the gilded mirror
hanging above the mantel, his expression grim as
he studied his reflection. The exertions of the day
had caused his hair to come loose from its queue
and it flowed past his collar in dark disarray, making him look even more like an unprincipled savage than ever. The rough-spun jacket he wore
when working the fields added to the illusion, and
his lips twisted in a bitter smile as he thought of
what his mother's guests would say if they were
to see him. *The Ox from Oxford*, he thought jeer-
ingly, and turned away from the mirror in disgust.

"It is just that both you and my mother are
right," he said at last, his gaze fixed on the toes of
his mud-splattered boots. "I am uncomfortable

with other people about, but that does not mean she should suffer for my faults." He raised his eyes and met Miss Haverall's gaze a second time. "Please assure her I want her to invite as many people as she pleases. I will manage somehow."

As the invitations had already been sent out, Portia considered his word most provident, and she turned her attention to the next part of her performance. "I can tell her anything you wish, sir," she said, shrugging her shoulders, "but I much doubt it will do any good. Unless your mother sees you act as if you are sincere in what you say, she is unlikely to invite anyone to Hawkshurst."

Connor frowned. "What do you mean?"

"I mean that, to quote Plutarch, 'Words are but the shadows of action,' " she returned with feigned coolness. "If you truly wish the countess to believe you are indifferent to whether or not she invites guests, then you must do everything within your power to convince her of that indifference."

"And how might I go about accomplishing that?" Connor demanded, silently cursing himself as he realized she was right. They hadn't had any houseguests since his mother's accident, and he was horrified to realize it had been because of him.

Portia busied herself refilling both their cups, unable to bear the silent anguish she could see shimmering in his forest-green eyes. Whatever the reasons for his misanthropy she knew they were far from frivolous, and for the first time since agreeing to help Lady Eliza, she knew a deep sense of shame. For a brief moment she was tempted to confess all and beg his forgiveness, but the thought of disappointing the countess was equally painful. Knowing she had no other choice, she pinned a thoughtful expression on her face as she handed him cup.

"Lady Alterwaithe will be arriving home within a sennight," she began carefully, as if she was only now considering the matter. "I would suggest that between now and then you make more of an effort to get out. Perhaps you might ride into town, or have a few of your friends over for a ride. You do have friends?" she asked quickly, paling at the horrifying possibility that he did not.

Despite his bleak thoughts, the expression on her face made Connor smile. "I am not such an ogre as to be a complete anathema to society," he assured her dryly. "I have several good friends, as it happens, although most of them are still in London attending Parliament."

"What of your neighbors?" she asked, thinking that if only he would smile more often the house would be filled to overflowing with ladies eager to catch his interest. "Surely there are a few of them you could invite over to tea?"

Connor thought of the local vicar and his plump, simpering wife. He usually invited them to visit a few times each year, knowing it was more or less expected of him. He'd had them in only last month, but he supposed he could tolerate their presence again if it would help convince his mother of his sincerity.

"The vicar and his good wife, I suppose," he provided with a marked lack of enthusiasm. "And while we're about it, we might as well invite Squire Hampson and his lady. There is a section of his land adjoining mine I have been meaning to discuss with him. It is perfect for raising sheep, but he has allowed it to lie fallow. Perhaps I could—"

"No," Portia interrupted with a firm shake of her head. "The taking of tea is a social occasion, and if your mama thinks you have invited the squire over to discuss farming we shall be right back where we started. Now, who else can we ask?"

"How many people do we need?" Connor demanded, annoyed to realize she was right. His mother was forever telling him he cared more for his land than anything else, and he was not about to risk proving her correct.

"More than four, certainly," she replied with a sniff, remembering the few times she had taken tea with members of the local gentry. "And we shall need some unattached young ladies and gentlemen to round out our numbers as well. Have you any suggestions?"

He wanted to suggest that they forget the whole bloody thing, but since he knew that would not do, Connor forced himself to consider the matter logically. "The Darlingtons on the next estate are nice enough," he said at last. "They have a half dozen daughters who are said to be stunners, and I know they stayed home this Season because they have only just come out of mourning for Mrs. Darlington's mother."

"Who else? We shall need several charming men if we are going to have a bevy of stunners in the parlor," Portia reminded him, wondering if anyone had ever referred to her as "a stunner." She doubted it. Usually people were too busy whispering about her hoydenish behavior to remark upon her looks.

Connor was about to snap that he was hardly a matchmaking mama who knew the name and location of every eligible man in the neighborhood when he suddenly remembered something.

"Keegan!" he exclaimed, his eyes shining at the thought of one of his oldest friends.

"Who?"

"The Honorable Keegan McLean, the younger son of the Earl of Camden," Connor said, beginning to look forward to the coming invasion of his home. "He lives in York when not in London, and I recall he mentioned he would be returning early. If he is in York he would be more than happy to attend, and I know we could count upon him to bring some friends with him. He is well-liked by everyone, and there is always a gaggle of young bucks hanging about him and clinging to his coattails. Shall I write him?"

"If you would, my lord," Portia said, stirring uneasily. His mentioning of coattails reminded her of the other part of her and the countess's plot, and she wondered how she would broach the subject. The matter was taken out of her hands a few moments later when the earl gave her a questioning look.

"Is there anything else, Miss Haverall?" he asked, his green gaze sharp. "Do you wish me to see to the refreshments as well?"

She tossed her head back, annoyed at his acuity. "The countess and I shall see to the food, your lordship," she retorted tartly. "All we require from you is that you put in an appearance."

"There must be more," Connor insisted, gauging from her reaction that he had struck a nerve. "Come, Miss Haverall," he urged when she remained stubbornly silent, "just say whatever it is you wish to say. I promise I shan't fly up into the boughs."

"It is your clothing," Portia blurted out, deciding to take him at his word. "You will forgive me, I am sure, but I could not help but notice that you . . .

that you . . ." Her voice trailed off, her cheeks flush-
ing with embarrassed color.

"That I what?" Connor asked, his tone deadly as
he set his cup to one side and crossed his arms
over his chest. "Pray do not stop now, ma'am. I
am finding this most illuminating. What precisely
about my wardrobe do you find so offensive that
it renders you speechless? The color, perhaps? Or
mayhap it is the cut you find so objectionable?
Please enlighten me."

"It is everything, if you must know!" Portia shot
back, deciding the arrogant beast didn't deserve
her sympathy. "The first thing I noticed about you
was that your clothes were poorly made and years
out of fashion. Indeed, the only thing I have seen
you wear that is even half way fashionable is your
riding clothes, and you can hardly wear *them* to
tea!"

"Indeed?" Connor's voice was frosty with fury.
"Then perhaps you are not as *au courant* with
fashion as you would like to believe. According
to the last issue of *Le Beau Monde*, wearing one's
riding togs in the drawing room is the latest
thing!"

"Perhaps, but only if the jackets are cut to fit,
and don't look as if they are about to burst at the
seams!" Portia retorted, and then covered her
mouth with her hand. She hadn't meant to say
that, and the look of pain that flashed across the
earl's face made her want to crawl off in shame.

"Oh, dear," she said, lowering her hand to her
lap and sending his lordship an apologetic look.
"What a dreadful cat you must think me. I am
sorry, my lord. I assure you it was not my intention to be so offensive."

Connor's anger faded at her obvious regret. "It
is I who ought to apologize to you, Miss Haverall," he said quietly. "I promised you I wouldn't

fly up in the boughs and then I all but bit off your nose when you but expressed your opinion. An opinion I myself solicited."

"Yes, but I didn't need to be so cutting," Portia insisted, still burning with remorse. "I hate it when other people snipe at me, regardless if I asked for their opinion or not. May I hope I haven't offended you beyond all bearing?" she asked tipping her head to one side and sending him a penitent look.

There was no way Connor could withstand so pretty an appeal, and he gave her a reluctant smile. "I am not offended," he said, retrieving his teacup from the side table and raising it to his lips. "Annoyed, perhaps, because you are right," he added with a flash of rueful honesty, "but I am not offended."

"Good." She gave a grateful sigh and turned her attention to her tea.

"What are you going to do about it?"

"Sir?" The non sequitur made her frown.

"My wardrobe," Connor reminded her, enjoying her look of confusion. "After castigating it as you did, I can only assume you were about to offer a solution. You were, weren't you?" he added when she continued staring at him blankly.

"Not precisely, my lord," she said, and then blushed furiously at the smug expression on his face. "That is, I was going to suggest you ask Mr. McLean for the name of his tailor, but that is all. If he lives in London, I am sure he must know what is all the crack."

"Oh, yes, Keegan is quite the dandy," Connor drawled, thinking of his elegant friend's fastidious nature. "But I hardly think a London tailor would do us any good."

"Perhaps not, but surely he must know the name of a local tailor? Someone in York, perhaps,"

Portia insisted, wishing she knew more of such matters. "We shall have to move fast if we hope to have you rigged out by next week."

"Next week?"

"The tea," she reminded him, eager to begin implementing her and the countess's careful scheme. "I was thinking Wednesday afternoon would be best. If that is all right with you?" She gave him an inquiring look.

He raised an eyebrow mockingly. "Do you mean I actually have a say in any of this?" he teased, amused at the efficient way she was taking command. She was rather like a filly who, with the bit firmly between her teeth, was determined to race headlong in whatever direction she chose.

"Certainly you have a choice." She scowled at him, annoyed by his obtuse behavior. "If Wednesday does not suit you, we can send out the invitations for Thursday."

Connor's lips twitched, but he was too wise to grin. "Wednesday is fine," he said, his voice as impassive as his expression. "Any particular time on Wednesday? I will need to know so that I might plan my day accordingly," he added innocently when she gave him a suspicious frown.

"Two o'clock," she said decisively, thinking that would be as good a time as any. "And I would also appreciate it if you would make yourself available for the next few afternoons."

"I should be delighted." He inclined his head with mock gravity. "Do you wish me to escort you into town?"

"Certainly not!" Portia laughed at the notion that she should require escort anywhere. "It is just that I wish you to be free."

"Free for what?" he wanted to know.

"Your fittings, of course," she said, as if to a

child. "The moment we learn the name of Mr. McLean's tailor I mean to send the man a note asking him to come to Hawkshurst at once. The sooner you are fitted for your new wardrobe, the better."

6

Two days later, Portia was hard at work in the study Lady Eliza had set aside for her use. The tea party had somehow become a garden party, and to her dismay the guest list had grown to include some thirty persons, and it showed no sign of stopping. She had tried mentioning her concerns to the countess, but the older woman had waved aside her objections.

"Nonsense, child, what is one person more or less?" she asked with a merry laugh. "Besides, as my mama-in-law use to say, ' 'Tis better to invite everybody than to risk offending anybody.' Just see to it, my dear, and I am sure all will be fine."

Portia was glad her ladyship was so optimistic, for she was beginning to experience serious trepidation regarding her ability to pull everything together in time. The staff was wonderful, thankfully, and even seemed to welcome the challenge of putting the house to rights. Even his lordship was cooperating . . . for him. Rather than wasting time with a letter, he'd ridden into York to visit his friend and returned with not only the name of Mr. McLean's tailor, but also a new valet, a small, delicately built man who went by the name of Samuels. He'd recently left the employ of a renowned dandy, and he had solemnly assured Portia he would make it his personal mission to bring his lordship "up to snuff," as he put it.

The weather was also cooperating, the cool, damp days giving way to warm sunlight and soft, summer breezes. The garden was a veritable riot of roses and pinks, and gazing out the window at the lavishly colored blossoms, Portia was forced to admit that everything was going remarkably well. The worries she were experiencing had little to do with the house, the guests, or even Lord Doncaster himself. The fault, as Shakespeare had so aptly put it, lay deep within herself.

She had been at Hawkshurst almost a fortnight, and with the exception of a few sharp exchanges with the earl, she had managed to behave with propriety. Lady Eliza was constantly praising her manners, and yesterday she had heard Mrs. Lester, the countess's housekeeper, remarking to one of the maids that she had never seen a sweeter young lady. But what would happen once there were other people about? she brooded, laying her forehead against the cool windowpane. Would she succeed in conducting herself with decorum and grace, or would she fall back on her old ways and shock everyone with her sharp tongue and unbecoming frankness?

It wasn't that she meant to misbehave, she assured herself anxiously; it was just that she'd never been able to twist herself into the mold society deemed proper for an unmarried young lady. Her father had taught her as he would have taught a son, and it wasn't until she was in her late teens that she discovered most people found her manner objectionable. Learning she was regarded as a quiz had stung her girlish pride, and she'd responded by behaving even more outrageously, delighting in her well-deserved reputation as a termagant.

But in the end she had paid a dear price for her defiance. Invitations had grown fewer and fewer in that last year, and with the exception of Lady Catherine DeClaire and Thomasina Perryvale, the new Duchess of Tilton, she had no true friends. Even her papa had turned against her, condemning her for the very traits he had instilled in her, and that had hurt more than anything she had ever deemed possible. She could not bear it if the same thing were to happen here.

She was standing at the window, still lost in her unhappy thoughts, when the sound of shouting gradually pierced her awareness. At first she thought the noise was coming from outside, and then she realized it was coming from the floor above her. What on earth . . . ? she thought, brows gathering in a frown as she started toward the door. She had just opened it and was peeking out into the hall when she saw the earl's newly hired tailor rushing down the stairs, his face flushed with temper.

"Never have I have been so insulted!" she heard him rage, his words ringing with indignation. "The townsfolk are right, the man is a monster! A barbarian! He is a philistine, and I refuse to squander my abilities on such as him!"

It took Portia less than a second to realize the significance of his dramatic statement, and she rushed out to stop him. "Monsieur André! Monsieur André! Please wait!" she called out, picking up her skirts and giving chase. "Do not go!"

The tailor turned at the bottom of the stairs, his cheeks pink with paint and fury. "I have sewn for kings!" he announced, shaking his tape at Portia. "For emperors! I have survived revolutions, wars, a dreadful winter in London that does not bear discussing, but I will not survive another moment in that man's company! I am going. Do not try to stop me!"

"But monsieur, what has happened?" Portia interposed herself between the irate man and the door. "I am sure this is all a silly misunderstanding, and—"

"I will tell you what happened," the earl's voice boomed out, and Portia looked up to see him leaning over the rail of the staircase. "That man-milliner wants to put me in stays!"

"They are not stays!" Monsieur André denied, tossing back his dark curls with a grace a girl might envy. "They are a device of my own design to hide the imperfections of my clients." He turned to Portia, who was trying not to laugh at the image of a scowling Lord Doncaster being laced into a corset.

"His lordship is too ... how shall I say ... *masculine* to wear my clothes," he said earnestly, his ebony eyes shining with fervor. "He is too broad here—" He patted his meager chest "—and too big here—" he indicated his slender shoulders "—to wear the jacket I have designed. I would have to sacrifice the lapels to ensure a proper fit, and that, mademoiselle, I refuse to do!"

Portia bit the inside of her cheek to keep from bursting into laughter. "I see," she said carefully, her voice shaking as she tried to compose herself. Lord Doncaster had come down the stairs, and if the wrathful scowl on his face was any indication, his mood was every bit as recalcitrant as monsieur's. Clearly a compromise of sorts was in order if she hoped to salvage the situation, and she forced herself to think logically.

"Perhaps you might design another jacket for his lordship," she suggested, giving the irate tailor a hopeful smile. "One with narrower lapels, or—"

"My jackets are known for their lapels!" Monsieur André interrupted, all but bristling with indignation. "To cut them by even a centimeter would be a desecration! I will not do it."

"Then perhaps a modified version of your ... er ... device," she suggested, trying another tactic, praying Lord Doncaster would cooperate—a hope that was quickly dashed by his furious response.

"I'm not wearing stays like an old woman!" he snapped, crossing his arms as he glared at both Portia and the tailor. He was wearing a white shirt of fine lawn, and the sight of his broad chest brought a flush to her cheeks.

"You see?" monsieur demanded of her, waving his tape like a battle pennant. "The man is an imbecile, with no sense of fashion. I wash my hands of him and this house!" And he turned toward the door.

"But monsieur, what of the earl's wardrobe?" Portia was desperate enough to plead. "We are having a garden party in a few days. What shall we do for clothes?"

The tailor whirled around and gave her a supercilious smirk. "Perhaps as mademoiselle presumes to tell André how to cut his jackets, she would prefer to design them herself?" he suggested with a sniff. "If so, you will need this." He tossed her the tape measure and stalked away, his beaked nose held high in the air.

"Of all the impudence ... " Lord Doncaster started forward, his jaw clenched with anger. Portia reached out and snagged him by the sleeve.

"Never mind, my lord," she said, her voice heavy with resignation. "It is no use trying to stop him. I fear he has already gone."

"Stop him?" he echoed, sending her an incredulous look. "I was going to help him on his way, preferably with my boot to his backside! If he ever dares set foot on Hawkshurst again, I shall have him shot!"

Although this was a sentiment Portia more than shared, she felt obliged to venture a gentle scold. "You shouldn't be so hard on the poor man, your lordship," she began in a firm voice. "He was but attempting to do his duty, and—" Her resolve and her voice both wavered. "Stays?" she asked, her eyes dancing with the laughter she could no longer suppress.

"They were sewn into the front of the jacket," he said, his lips beginning to twitch as well. "An ingenious device, I grant you, but dashed uncomfortable. When I put the wretched thing on I couldn't so much as draw a breath." He grinned down at her, his tone provocative as he added, "Now I know what you poor ladies endure in the name of fashion. You have my undying sympathy, I promise you."

His warm tone and the gleam in his eyes brought Portia to a sudden awareness of their positions. Her hand was resting on his muscled forearm, and he was standing so close to her she could feel his warm breath against her cheek. She dropped her hand and took a discreet step away from him.

"Well, it seems we are right back where we started," she said, her light tone hiding her inner turmoil. "The garden party is in less than a week, and you've not so much as a decent shirt to your name."

Connor gave her a thoughtful look, taking in the delightful flush on her cheeks and the way her eyes would not quite meet his. He knew he should follow her example and excuse himself, but he was oddly averse to do so. Standing so near to her, he could catch the soft scent of her perfume, and he allowed himself the luxury of inhaling her sweet fragrance before moving reluctantly away.

"Come, ma'am, you are being unconscionably hard on my wardrobe," he teased, matching his tone to hers. "Things are not quite so bleak as *that*."

"As good as," she said, and then gave him a considering look, as if only now noticing he was in his shirtsleeves. "Although that shirt you are wearing seems adequate enough."

"Than I shall wear it, and nothing else," he said, some imp of mischief goading him on. "Perhaps I shall set a new fashion amongst the gentlemen."

The color in her cheeks intensified. "A short-lived fashion, if the ladies have anything to do with it!" she snapped, furious with herself for being affected by his boldness. "The thought of unclothed gentlemen in the parlor is not to be borne!"

"Unclothed gentlemen?" he repeated, his eyes round with mock incredulity. "You shock me, Miss Haverall, indeed you do. *I* was but suggesting I do without my jacket. Whatever did you think I meant?" He added this last with such patent innocence that Portia gave a soft laugh.

"Wretch!" she accused, the harsh word belied by the smile on her lips. "I am serious, you know. You need new clothes."

"I do not see why," he said, taking her arm and guiding her into the parlor. "I have a wardrobe full of clothes I've not worn in years. Won't they do?"

"Only if you want people to take you for a quiz." Portia sighed, shaking her head at the foibles of men. "Ah, well, I suppose we've really no choice; they will have to suffice until we can find you another tailor."

"If he is anything like the last one, you may

spare yourself the effort," he said firmly, all but cringing in repugnance. "I refuse to have another tulip like that fluttering about me."

"Then what do you suggest we do?" Portia queried, annoyance beginning to affect her usual enjoyment of the ridiculous. She and Lady Eliza were both going to a great deal of effort on the earl's behalf, and it seemed to her the least he could do was to take some effort with his appearance.

Her sharp tone made Connor's eyebrows arch. He'd been about to suggest they send to York for another tailor and pay him double to stitch something up, but now he was hanged if he would say a single word. Instead he lounged against the mantel, his manner indifferent as he sent her a cool look. "I haven't the slightest idea, Miss Haverall," he challenged, neatly returning the ball to her court. "What do *you* suggest?"

Portia's hands clenched, and for a moment she was wildly tempted to tell him he could take his blasted jackets and feed them to the pigs. The words even formed on her lips, but she bit them back with herculean effort. Her days of saying whatever she pleased were behind her, she told herself sternly, and regardless of the temptation, she would control her tongue.

Very well, she thought, her foot tapping out an impatient tattoo as she considered the matter of the earl's wardrobe. What would she do? Since the garden party was looming, a proper day coat and breeches were clearly the most pressing priority; everything else could wait. She weighed all the options available to her, arriving at what she considered the best solution for all.

"I suggest we have Samuels look through your wardrobe and choose the least offensive items," she said slowly, working out the matter as she spoke. "Then we can have your mother's modiste perform whatever alterations are necessary to bring them up to current fashions." She folded her arms, and gave him a look as if daring him to object. "What do you say, my lord?"

Her cleverness impressed Connor, and he had to concede her plan was a good one. Not that he was about to admit as much, of course. Instead he pretended to consider the notion, his mouth pursing in a thoughtful frown as he regarded her.

"I am not certain I care for the idea of that any more than I liked having that French fop flitting about me," he said at last, moving his shoulders in a dismissive shrug. "You shall have to think of something else."

Portia, who had expected him to accept her idea with suitable gratitude, scowled in annoyance. "Why should I want to do that?" she demanded. " 'Tis the perfect solution, and you know it!"

He decided to grant her that much, although he still feigned obstinacy. "I am not having that hen-witted female take my measurements," he stated, chin firming as he gave her his coldest look. That look had been known to make grown men quake with fright, but he was pleased to see it had no discernible effect on her. Indeed, she looked as if she'd like nothing better than to hit him over the head with another bed warmer.

"All right then, perhaps Samuels could—"

"No," he interrupted, enjoying himself to the hilt. "He is nice enough, but he puts me too much in mind of Monsieur André."

She shot him a look fairly dripping with scorn. "Then who do you suggest, my lord?" she snapped caustically. "Williams?"

The idea of the rigidly proper butler performing what he would surely deem a menial task almost made Connor laugh aloud. He knew he had teased her long enough, and was about to agree to whatever she wished when he noticed she was still holding the measuring tape Monsieur André had hurled at her. He stared at it for a moment, a roguish plan forming in his mind. He raised his gaze to find her watching him, and gave her a slow smile.

"If you are so determined to rig me out like some simpering dandy," he drawled, his eyes full of challenge, "*you* may do the honors."

To his amusement she turned a rosy hue. "Lord Doncaster!"

"You object?" he asked, as if surprised.

"Certainly I object," she sputtered. " 'Tis the most improper thing I have ever heard!"

"And you, of course, would never dream of doing anything improper," he returned, nodding his head as if in agreement. "Very well, Miss Haverall, as I have no desire to put you to the blush we shall forget this entire conversation took place. Now if you will excuse me, I shall return to my room." He pushed himself away from the mantel as if to go.

"But what about your wardrobe?" she asked, chewing her lip and regarding him with marked suspicion.

"What about it?" he asked, shrugging his shoulders indifferently. "*I* am not the one who finds it so objectionable. If you are not prepared to remedy the situation, then there is nothing left to say."

Portia stared at him, torn between disbelief and sheer temper. The wretch! He had no intention of having her measure him for a new wardrobe; he was only using her refusal as an excuse not to co-operate! Well, she decided, her lips thinning as she saw the smug satisfaction in his green eyes, they would see about that!

"As you wish, my lord," she said calmly, lifting

her eyes to meet his. "If you would be so good as to hold your arms out at your sides, I shall begin."

Her boldness shocked Connor almost as much as it delighted him. He'd expected her either to blush and stammer in embarrassment, or to toss the tape in his face and tell him to go to the devil. That she had done neither intrigued him, and he decided it would be interesting to see how far she was prepared to go. Hiding a smile, he crossed the room to stand before her.

"Like this, do you mean?" he drawled, holding his arms out as she had bade him.

The sight of his massive chest and muscled arms inches from her nose made the breath catch in Portia's throat. The only other man she'd seen in his shirtsleeves was her father, and he had looked nothing like his lordship. Indeed, she thought, swallowing self-consciously, she found it difficult to believe any man could look half so vital as the earl. She clutched the measuring tape, drawing a deep breath for comfort before meeting his gaze with as much equanimity as she could muster.

"I will need pen and paper so that I can write down your measurements," she said, her voice wooden as she ordered herself not to blush.

"Top drawer," he said, nodding at the elegant writing desk in front of the narrow windows. "Mother usually keeps her stationery there."

Grateful for the chance to leave his disturbing presence, she hurried across the room to retrieve the needed items. When she returned, the earl was regarding her with such a look of innocence that she was instantly suspicious.

"Where do you wish to start?" he asked, his deep voice rich with laughter and challenge.

She glared at him, wishing the tape was a garrote so that she could have the pleasure of throttling him. "The neck, I suppose," she said with a singular lack of enthusiasm, stepping closer and raising her arms to loop the tape about his tanned throat.

He was so tall she had to stand on her toes to put the pieces of tape together, and the action brought her even closer to his muscular body. She could feel the warmth of his skin, and smell the crisp, masculine scent of the cologne he favored, and the sensations made her concentration waver. Unbidden, she found herself wondering what it would be like if those strong arms hanging loosely at his side were to close about her and . . .

"Not so tight, if you please," he protested, wincing slightly as she tightened her hold on the tape. "I have no wish to be strangled."

"A tempting thought," she muttered darkly, gritting her teeth when he gave a rich chuckle in response.

"What next?" he asked, his gaze resting on her as she stepped back to jot down the numbers.

Portia's fingers tightened on the quill. "Your . . . your chest," she said, unable to meet his eyes. This was proving even harder than she imagined, and she was strongly tempted to admit defeat. Only the knowledge that such cowardice would doubtlessly delight him kept her from doing just that, and she mentally stiffened her spine as she turned back to him.

She kept her manner brisk and her face blank as she reached around him, ignoring the racing of her heart. The rising and falling of his chest was almost as big a distraction as the cloud of dark hair she could see beneath the thin fabric of his shirt, but she stoically paid them no mind. Finally it was over, and she uttered a silent prayer as she wrote down the last figure.

"Here you are, my lord," she said, eyes averted

as she handed him the piece of paper. "You may present these to the modiste."

"Do you mean to say we are finished?" he asked, eyes mocking as his fingers closed around the paper. "What of the rest of my clothing? As you have already pointed out, I can hardly appear in society dressed only in a shirt."

Portia took his meaning at once. "I am sure your valet is far more capable of finishing the task, my lord," she muttered, willing herself not to blush.

He gave her a wicked grin. "More capable, perhaps," he conceded in that low, mocking voice she was coming to recognize, "but I doubt I would enjoy the experience nearly as much."

Her face flamed red, and she threw the tape in his face. "You may go the devil!" she exclaimed, almost hating him in that moment. The sound of his laughter followed her as she fled from the room, and she vowed furiously that if it was the last thing she did, she would make him pay for his mockery.

The day of the garden party dawned cool and gray, the heretofore blue skies leaden with the promise of rain. Portia stood in front of the French doors leading out into the gardens, her expression as stormy as the weather as she stared out at the tables and chairs she and the staff had spent most of yesterday arranging. The thought that all of their efforts were for naught was most disheartening, but she brushed her disappointment aside and began formulating alternate plans should the worst occur. She was weighing the possibility of moving the festivities to the orangery when she heard the countess's Bath chair behind her. She turned just as the countess, pushed by a footman, entered the room.

"Never say it is raining!" Lady Eliza exclaimed in disgust, dismissing the footman.

"Not yet, but I fear it may before the afternoon is over," Portia said with a sigh, moving away from the window. "Ah, well, I suppose it was too much to expect the good weather to hold."

"What nonsense. We often have beautiful weather this time of year. This is all your fault!" Lady Eliza retorted, fixing Portia with a dark scowl.

"My fault?" Portia repeated, stung by the accusation.

"Certainly. If you had invited the vicar, as Connor suggested, this would never have happened. It never does to insult God, you know."

The waspish reply made Portia laugh. "You are the one who said the man was an unmitigated bore," she reminded the countess, moving to sit at her desk. "And for your information, my lady, I did invite the good vicar. He and his wife will be here along with the rest of your neighbors."

"Hmmmph. So we will be preached to death as well as rained upon," Lady Eliza grumbled, drumming her fingers on the handle of her chair. "I must say this is vexing; nothing is going as I had hoped it would."

The surprising observation made Portia glance up from the list she had been perusing. "Whatever do you mean?" she asked, puzzled and more than a little hurt by the countess's words. She'd worked very hard on the party, and she thought everything had been going remarkably well.

The countess saw the hurt on Portia's face and gave a self-deprecatory shrug. "Oh, dear, I hadn't meant to sound quite so critical," she apologized. "You have done an excellent job of arranging this party, and I am quite sure it will be a wonderful success. It is just that I am worried about Connor."

Portia stiffened at the sound of the earl's name. In the days since the incident in the parlor she had gone out of her way to avoid him, and when she could not, she treated him with stilted civility. He seemed to find her efforts most amusing, and more than once she had longed to slap the knowing smile from his lips. Arrogant devil, she brooded resentfully. Whatever had made her think him a cold fish? He was a teasing, provoking beast, and she was still determined to exact her revenge on him. All that remained was deciding where and how she would do it.

Realizing the countess was waiting for her reply, Portia bestirred herself and gave the older woman a look of polite inquiry. "What of his lordship?" she asked, pleased with her cool tone. "There isn't a problem with his wardrobe, is there?"

"No, thank heaven," the countess said with a relieved sigh. "In fact, the lad has seldom looked better. That valet of his is a wonder with a thread and needle, and he has brought several of Connor's jackets up to crack. No, 'tis not the clothes themselves that bother me; rather 'tis the man inside those clothes."

Portia gaped at Lady Eliza in amazement. However angry she might be at his lordship, she still admired him, and she found it difficult to imagine him doing anything to bring disgrace on himself or his family name.

"What does your ladyship mean?" she asked, striving to understand the countess's worry.

Lady Eliza gave another sigh. "You do not know Connor as well as I do," she said, her eyes sad as they met Portia's gaze. "He is not nearly as sanguine about this party as he lets on."

"I know he only agreed to it to please you," Portia said slowly, recalling the earl's initial resistance to the idea, "but since then he has been most helpful. Indeed, it was his suggestion that we use the small tents to protect the food from the heat and the insects."

"Oh, yes, Connor would do whatever he thought was required of him, regardless of how painful it might be," the other woman said with a humorless laugh. "He is much like his father in that respect. But that doesn't mean he is looking forward to this afternoon with anything other than dread."

"But why?" Portia was confused. Admittedly the party was bound to be a dead bore for a worldly man like Doncaster, but she sensed the countess meant something far more serious than a simple case of ennui.

The countess hesitated as if uncertain what to say. She threaded her fingers together, her expression anxious as she studied Portia's face. "We never mention the matter, even amongst ourselves," she said in solemn tones, "but I know it is because of this tragic incident in his past that Connor has hidden himself on our estate. He would be furious if he knew I have told you, but I feel you have the right to know."

"Thank you, my lady," Portia replied, steeling herself to hear the details of some dreadful scandal. It was a duel, she decided, easily envisioning the earl with a pistol in his hand, his green eyes full of icy calm as he faced his opponent. The earl had killed his man, and now he was an outcast from society.

Or perhaps it was an affair, she amended, recalling the devastating charm his lordship could wield when it suited him. Yes, he had gone mad for a married lady, and the woman's husband had threatened scandal. Perhaps he had even called Connor out, and he had no choice but to accept. Perhaps . . .

"It began the year he turned twenty-one, and his papa and I insisted he come to London for the Season," Lady Eliza began, her expression pensive as she lost herself in the past. "He'd always resisted before, claiming he couldn't leave his books or his duties on the estate. He is so very conscientious, you know, just like his father, and usually he would do whatever was asked of him without question."

As Portia had already experienced the earl's dedication to duty firsthand, she could readily believe his mother's glowing praise. But as she was still annoyed with him, she was unwilling to give the devil his due. "Mayhap he was enjoying himself too much to leave," she said, lowering her gaze to the papers piled on her desk.

The countess shook her head with a soft laugh. "It wasn't that at all!" she replied. "I know you would not credit it to look at him, but while he was at Oxford Connor was dreadfully bookish. He preferred his studies to the ladybirds and carousing ... quite unlike his father when I first met him, I might add."

Portia winced, recalling the morning at the ruins when his lordship had demonstrated his obvious expertise. "But you say you were able to persuade him to go to London?" she asked, hiding her shame behind the gruff question.

"Yes, and almost from the start it was an unmitigated disaster."

That brought Portia's head up with a snap. "A disaster?" she echoed in disbelief.

"It is his size, you see," Lady Eliza explained with an earnest look. "He has always been so much taller than most of the men, and he simply *towers* over the ladies. People would stare so whenever he entered a room, and I fear it made him dreadfully self-conscious."

The idea of Doncaster being anything other than supremely arrogant would have been laughable in any other situation, but Portia didn't feel like laughing. "It is rather difficult to imagine his lordship being self-conscious," she said, her heart aching for the earl. "He always seems so sure of himself."

"And so he is . . . now," the countess agreed with a sigh. "But this was when he was younger, and uncertain of himself in social situations. He tried, but the more people stared and whispered, the more he withdrew into himself. We could hardly get him to accept any invitations, and just when things were looking their bleakest he met *that woman.*"

"What woman?" Portia asked, wondering if her original suspicions were correct, and the earl had indulged in an illicit affair.

"Miss Olivia Carlisle, the niece of the Earl of Stamford," Lady Eliza provided, her mouth thinning in anger. "She was the toast of London, all blonde curls and dimpled smiles, a perfect pocket Venus. The blades all went mad for her, including Connor. He offered for her, and do you know what that hussy did?"

"As his lordship has no wife, I would gather she refused him," Portia replied, hiding her surprise that a mere niece of an earl would have turned down so eligible a *parti* as his lordship. Unless the lady had bigger fish already on her string, she added to herself, wondering what had become of the young woman.

"Ha! That was only the half of it! She *laughed* at him, saying she would as lief marry her mother's footman as tie herself to him. She called him . . . Oh! I can not say it!" Lady Eliza's eyes flashed with fury. "Even a dozen years later the memory of her vile insult makes my blood boil!"

Portia blinked in astonishment. "Good heavens, ma'am!" she said, trying to imagine what Miss Carlisle could have said to have so enraged the usually placid countess. "Whatever did she call him?"

"She called him by the cruelest of nicknames," the countess raged. "The name she herself had given him. She called him the Ox from Oxford!"

7

"The what?"

"The Ox from Oxford," Lady Eliza repeated in a clipped voice. "The little baggage named him that after he fell and broke a table at Almack's. Not that it was his fault, mind," she added anxiously. "Another man tripped him, accidentally *he* claimed, but it was poor Connor who took the blame."

"That is terrible," Portia said, understanding now the earl's remarks that day at the ruins. No wonder he had such a poor opinion of her sex, she mused sadly. A sudden thought occurred to her, and she sent the countess a curious look.

"Whatever became of Miss Carlisle?" she asked, hoping to hear the chit had met with some terrible misfortune.

The countess gave a haughty sniff. "She married the Marquis of Duxford," she said in a voice dripping with scorn. "the man was old enough to have been her father, but he had more than enough gold to make up for his advanced years. Now that he's finally popped off, I hear she is on the catch for a new title. 'Tis rumored she will be visiting the Bowlands later this summer, and I am praying she won't bother us. It shall be difficult enough getting Connor to cooperate with our plans, but if he should learn she is lurking about, well, I needn't tell you what *that* would portend!"

"Indeed you do not, my lady," Portia replied, easily envisioning the earl's possible reaction to the news. "Still, I feel it might be better if we at least mention it to him. That way he won't be taken by surprise should he encounter her. 'Forewarned is forearmed,' you know."

"Perhaps, but if Connor even suspects that minx is in the neighborhood he will likely hole up like a badger in his den." Lady Eliza's expression was stern as she met Portia's gaze. "You must promise you shan't say a word to him."

Portia was uncertain what she should do. She certainly had no desire to defy the countess, but neither did she wish to deceive his lordship. Instinct told her he would not appreciate being kept in the dark, and she could imagine his fury should he learn the truth. On the other hand, she did not see why she should upset him unless it was absolutely necessary.

"Very well, my lady, I shall do as you ask. But," she cautioned when the countess would have spoken, "if Lady Duxford does stay with her friends, then I insist his lordship be told. It is only fair."

Lady Eliza opened her mouth as if to disagree, and then closed it again. "As you wish, my dear," she said, inclining her head in approval. "Now that we have resolved that matter, there is something else I should like to discuss with you."

"What is that, ma'am?"

"I have decided that instead of introducing you as my companion, I shall introduce you as my guest," Lady Eliza said in a decisive tone. "And 'tis more or less the truth when you think about it. Georgianne did write granting you permission to stay with us, you know."

Portia cringed, recalling the letter her great-aunt

had written the countess some two days earlier. The elderly lady had learned of the incident at the inn, and if the three-page tirade was to be believed, she was far from amused. She had informed Lady Eliza that if she wanted "the little hoyden" to remain with them, then she was welcome to her. She also added a cold postscript that should Portia learn to conduct herself in a manner befitting a proper lady, she was free to return to the bosom of her family. Until then, it was strongly suggested she might find the wilds of Yorkshire more to her liking.

"That is very kind of you, my lady," Portia said, shaking off the remnants of old pain as she smiled at the countess. "But I do not care if people know I am your companion. That is why Lord Doncaster brought me here, after all."

"You may not care, but I do," the countess answered with surprising vehemence. "People, even good people, tend to treat companions and poor relations as if they are invisible, and I'll not have you snubbed by our guests. Believe me," she added grimly, "I fully know whereof I speak."

"Oh?" Portia was intrigued by the confession.

The countess shook her head. "It is an old story, child, and a long one. Someday when we have more time I promise to tell you all, but in the meanwhile I believe I shall go to my rooms for a little nap."

Portia rose to her feet and moved over to the countess's chair. "Shall I push you to the steps, my lady?" she asked, placing her hands on the chair's lacquered handles.

"If you wish," the countess agreed, closing the leather apron that covered her lower limbs. "It will be quicker than sending for the footman."

"I've often wondered why you do not use a wheelchair," Portia remarked as she guided the chair with its two large back wheels and smaller front wheel through the door. "They're much smaller, and you wouldn't need to depend on others to push you about."

"I'd thought of it." Lady Eliza surprised Portia with her admission. "But I didn't wish to offend the servants."

"How would your buying a wheelchair offend them?"

The countess gave an unhappy sigh. "They were all so upset when I had that silly fall," she muttered. "They could not do enough for me, and if I attempted to do the smallest thing for myself they acted so hurt. I vow, if I'd had any idea the entire household would be thrown into such chaos by all this, I'd have never—" She broke off abruptly.

"Never what, my lady?"

"Never tried to take that silly fence, of course," Lady Eliza finished with a light laugh. "But that is pride for you. In my case, it truly went before a fall. Ah, there is John!" she exclaimed, summoning the stocky footman with a wave of her hand.

"Will there be anything else, Lady Doncaster?" Portia asked, watching as the footman lifted the countess from her chair.

"Heavens, no!" the older woman replied, giving her a quick smile. "Just try to relax, my dear, and pray the party doesn't end in disaster. That is all any of us can do."

"If your lordship will kindly refrain from squirming, I shall have this thing tied in a moment," Samuels pleaded, swaying on tiptoe as he added the finishing touches to Connor's cravat. "It needs only one more tug, and . . . there! Perfection!"

While the smaller man stepped back to admire his creation, Connor turned to the mirror, half-afraid of what he would see. The sight that greeted him made him blink in pleasant surprise.

Instead of the frilly, uncomfortable monstrosities he remembered from his youth, the cravat his valet had fashioned was a simple arrangement of starched white linen. The folds lay flat against the front of his shirt, and instead of extending past his ears, the points of his collar barely brushed his chin. He'd also allowed Samuels to cut his hair, and even to his critical eyes, the effect was pleasing. Perhaps this afternoon wouldn't be the torment he dreaded, he thought, tugging on the cuffs of his shirt.

"Is everything all right, my lord?" Samuels asked anxiously, brushing a fleck of lint from the shoulders of Connor's black jacket. "Is the coat not to your liking?"

"No, it's fine, Samuels," Connor said, and was shocked to realize it was true. He'd always hated the fashionable clothes his mother insisted he wear, feeling as if he was suffocating every time he pulled on one of the tight satin jackets she had claimed were *de rigueur* for a gentleman.

"I was afraid the lapels would be too narrow," the valet continued, fretting and fussing as he helped Connor finish his toilet. "But now I think they are just right. Your lordship's chest is much too broad for wide lapels."

Remembering Monsieur André's refusal to compromise the width of his lapels, he was strongly tempted to tease his too-serious valet on the matter. Then he studied his reflection again, and a new concern arose to plague him.

"Are you quite certain the gentlemen wear their pantaloons this tight?" he asked, giving his yellow nankins an anxious look. He had ordered them made last year, but Samuels had insisted upon altering them, commenting with a sniff that a *gentleman* would never wear so ill-fitting a garment. They were not ill-fitting now, Connor thought, turning for a better look at his reflection. Indeed, they fit as smoothly as a riding glove, the soft fabric hugging his thighs to an embarrassing degree.

Samuels gave him a long-suffering look that was beginning to become familiar. "Pantaloons must be tight to give a gentleman the proper silhouette," he said, with the studied patience of a tutor addressing a slow-witted pupil. "You look quite dashing, my lord, I assure you. The ladies shall swoon when they see you."

Connor's jaw clenched at the soothing words. "Let us hope not, Samuels. I should hate to think we have gone through all of this for nothing." He gave his reflection one last glance, and then turned and left the room.

He went downstairs to find all in chaos, servants running madly about like a group of ants whose nest had been disturbed. A few sharp questions to his distracted housekeeper brought an annoyed scowl to his face, and he stormed out to the garden in search of the perpetrator. He found her standing beside the refreshment tents, snapping off orders with all the skill of a top sergeant. He stalked over to her just as she was directing that a pot of his mother's favorite pinks be carried into the house.

"What the devil is going on here?" he demanded, brows meeting in a threatening scowl as he glowered down at her. "I thought this was going to be a garden party!"

"As did I, my lord, but it would seem God has other ideas," came Miss Haverall's unrepentant reply as she turned to face him. "Your guests will hardly be pleased if we allow them to be caught in a deluge."

Connor could see the wisdom of her words, but such understanding in no way mollified him. He'd steeled himself to suffer through a garden party, and the sudden change of plans left him feeling strangely vulnerable. He brushed aside the unwelcome sensation in annoyance, turning his displeasure on the only person available.

"Shouldn't you wait before rain actually begins falling before you admit defeat?" he asked irritably. "You went to a great deal of trouble to arrange this thing, and it seems foolish to undo everything because of a few harmless clouds."

A flash of lightning split the sky as if in reply, followed quickly by a roll of thunder. Miss Haverall crossed her arms and gave him an arch look. "Harmless?" she repeated in a dulcet tone that was at odds with the gleam in her eyes.

Connor tried not to laugh, but in the end he was unable to hold back a wry chuckle. "Very well, ma'am, I surrender," he said, giving her a low bow. "I refuse to argue with both you and the Almighty. Move the entire garden inside, if that is your pleasure."

"Your lordship is too generous," she answered, her lips curving in appreciation, "but I want only the appearance of a garden, not the reality. A few pinks and roses will suffice, I promise you."

As if by unspoken agreement they began walking back toward the house. They'd gone only a few paces when Connor remarked, "Why did you decide to move the party into the house, if I might ask? I thought it was agreed the orangery was to be used in the event the weather played us false."

"That was my original plan," Miss Haverall admitted, "but after careful consideration I decided it would be better if we moved everything into the house. That way the guests can make use of the music or game room if they so desire."

It made sense, and Connor nodded in agreement. "Clever and cool-minded as always, Miss Haverall. I might have known you knew precisely what you were about. My apologies for snapping at you as I did."

To his relief she gave a light laugh. "You are certainly entitled to be displeased with the disruption of your household," she said, tilting her head and giving him a teasing smile. The smile suddenly vanished, and she gave him such an odd look that he was instantly apprehensive.

"What is wrong?"

"You are wearing a new jacket," she blurted out, and then blushed at her boldness. She looked so chagrined, in fact, that Connor's wariness vanished at once.

"It is one of my old ones, actually. Samuels altered it for me," he said, trying not to preen with pride. "Do you like it?"

"It looks wonderful!" she exclaimed, her voice filled with admiration. "And that cravat is marvelous! An American, is it not?"

Connor stroked the front of his stock, too ashamed to confess his ignorance of such matters. To him the cravat was nothing more than an uncomfortable bother, and he didn't care what the style might be.

"I believe so," he replied, deciding it was the safest response. Anxious for a new topic of conversation he turned to her, taking note of her appearance with appreciation.

"May I say you are also looking quite dashing?" he said with a charming smile. "That is a new gown, is it not?"

She gave a melodic laugh. "No, like yours it is one of my older garments. I had it made shortly before my father died, but this is the first opportunity I have had to wear it."

He gave her another admiring look, saying the first words to enter his head. "The color becomes you."

Her cheeks grew as rosy as her muslin gown. "Thank you, sir, it is most kind of you to say so."

Connor frowned slightly. His compliment had been sincere. "I was not being kind, ma'am," he began, "I—"

"Oh, look!" she interrupted, quickening her pace. "Williams is giving us the evil eye. Your guests must be arriving, and we are not there to greet them. He will think us shockingly lax in our duties."

An icy fear settled in Connor's stomach, and the cravat, which had fit so comfortably only moments before, now seemed unbearably tight. The thought of jumping on his horse and riding as far as he could was sweetly tempting, but he sternly suppressed it. He was a Doncaster, he reminded himself proudly, and Doncasters did not run. His father had stood unmoving in the face of enemy fire at Cowpens, and he'd be hanged if he'd break rank and flee because of a few old women and simpering girls. He drew his shoulders back, his hand tightening slightly on Miss Haverall's elbow as he marched forward to meet his fate.

"So you are Miss Haverall," the elderly woman said, her pale-blue eyes narrowing as they rested on Portia's face. "Can't say as I've heard the name before. Are you in society?"

"No, Mrs. Goodkin, I am not," Portia replied in a stiff voice, wishing the disagreeable old biddy would go off and find someone else to pester. She had been trapped with the squire's mother-in-law

for the past quarter hour, and she could feel her
small store of patience evaporating. Another five
minutes in the woman's company, and she would
not be held responsible for whatever she might
say . . . or do, she added silently, casting a longing
look at the punch bowl.

"I thought not." Satisfaction dripped from Mrs.
Goodkin as she raised her punch glass to her lips
for a noisy gulp. "At first I thought you might be
another of dear Lady Eliza's companions, but
when she assured me you are here as her guest, I
must admit I was stymied. However did you
meet?"

*When I bashed her son over the head with a bed
warmer,* Portia thought, wondering what the older
woman's reaction would be if she were to admit to
the truth. Doubtlessly she would swoon with horror, and then go dashing off to spread the gossip
once she had recovered, Portia decided with a
scornful smirk.

"Her ladyship is an old friend of my great-aunt,
the Countess of Lowton," she said instead, raising
her chin and giving Mrs. Goodkin a superior look.
"Perhaps you have heard of *her?*"

Mrs. Goodkin's jowly face turned a mottled red.
"I believe I may have," she muttered, her gaze
sliding away from Portia's. She glanced around
the crowded drawing room, brightening visibly as
her gaze came to rest on a woman in an atrocious
ensemble of purple and gold silk.

"I see my neighbor, Mrs. Fashingham, over
there talking to our hostess," she said, already
pushing herself to her feet. "If you will excuse me,
Miss Haverall, I believe I shall go over and have a
word with her."

"Must you go so soon? How sad," Portia cooed,
delighted at having achieved her objective with so
little effort.

Other than a sharp look, Mrs. Goodkin gave no indication she had caught the sarcasm in Portia's voice, and Portia was left in blissful solitude. Content, she settled back against her chair, her eyes bright with pleasure as she gazed slowly about her.

It was all going quite well, she thought, satisfaction spreading through her. Her decision to move the party indoors had proven a good one, as rain had begun falling minutes after the last guest to arrive had made his bows. The guests took the change of location in stride, and other than a pair of blonde beauties who were obviously put out not to be able to wear their pretty new bonnets, everyone seemed to be having a good time. Or almost everyone, she amended with a sigh, her gaze coming to rest on the earl.

He was standing in the corner by the fireplace, his posture rigid, and a cold, unapproachable look stamped on his handsome face. Every now and then one of the braver guests would venture over for a word with him, but she noted they never stayed very long. What on earth was wrong with the wretch? she wondered, her brows gathering as she watched him rout yet another intrepid guest.

It was as if he was deliberately trying to drive people away, yet why should he wish to do that? He could be charming when he wanted to, and certainly he never seemed to lack for conversation when the two of them were together. Indeed, his remarks about her gown were quite witty and his conduct in the drawing room when she was measuring him for his new shirt bordered on the flirtatious. If he could act like that with her, she reasoned with a decisive nod, then he could act like that with the rest of the guests!

Her mind made up, she rose to her feet and walked over to where he was standing. His wariness vanished at once, and his dark-green eyes lost their icy sheen as he greeted her.

"All seems to be going quite well, Miss Haverall," he said with a cool nod. "If there is anything I can do to be of assistance, please let me know."

Portia fought the urge not to screech at such obtuse behavior. He hadn't made so much as a single move to mingle with the guests, and yet he had the effrontery to ask if he could be of assistance . . . ! Had any other man made the same offer she would have accused him of sarcasm. "If your lordship truly wishes to be of service," she snapped, lowering her voice to avoid being overheard, "you can stop acting like a suit of armor that has strayed from the main hall, and start acting more like a host!"

His lips lost their warm smile, and he drew himself up even taller. "I do not know what you mean, ma'am," he denied in a stiff voice, his eyes flashing with fury. "I have been a perfect host. I greeted every guest, did I not?"

"Yes, and with all the enthusiasm of an Egyptian being visited by yet another plague!" she returned, chin coming up as she faced him. "You haven't so much as approached a single guest since the party began, and the few guests who have dared approach you, you sent packing!" She shook her head in disgust. "No wonder people look at you as if you are an ogre; that is how you behave!"

His face grew even colder. "If you think I mean to caper about like a fool, then you are much mistaken."

If he had glowered at Miss Montgomery like that, Portia could see why the hapless creature had run screaming into the night. Fortunately she was made of sterner stuff, and instead of fleeing, she simply folder her arms across her chest and met him glare for glare.

"What I expect, sir," she said in the tone she had often used when arguing with her papa, "is that you do your duty. And you may begin with that lady." She nodded at a modestly attired young woman sitting on the far side of the room.

Connor burned at the insult to his honor, but what burned more was the knowledge that she was right. He fought back his anger and forced himself to concentrate on the woman Miss Haverall had indicated. "Who is she?" he asked, struggling to recall the lady's name.

"Miss Felicity DeCamp," Portia provided, breathing a silent sigh of relief that he hadn't taken umbrage at her words. "She is visiting her cousins, the Brextons, and she doesn't know a soul here. As her host, it is your responsibility to see she is comfortable, and that she doesn't fade into a wallflower."

Connor eyed the delicate blonde with trepidation. "She looks as if she'd swoon if a man so much as gave her a cross look," he said, recalling what had happened the last time he had approached a shy young lady.

"Then don't give her one," Portia advised with a none-too-gentle prod. "Come now, you have dawdled long enough."

They crossed the room and were soon standing in front of Miss DeCamp, who stared up at them with wide, velvet-brown eyes.

"Good afternoon, Miss DeCamp," Portia said, offering the other woman a warm smile. "I believe you have met our host, Lord Doncaster. I was just telling his lordship you were from Bath, and he was remarking on the many Roman ruins in the area. Roman antiquities are something of hobby of his lordship's," she added in what she hoped was an encouraging manner.

The brown eyes widened in surprise. "They are?" she said, giving Connor a shy look. "They are also an interest of mine. We found a Roman statue in our pasture, you know."

"Indeed?" That piqued Connor's interest. He had heard much of the Roman ruins being unearthed about Bath, and he had been toying with the idea of going down for a look. "Which god?"

"We believe it is a representation of the emperor Claudius," Miss DeCamp said, her quiet demeanor becoming more animated. "The statue is wearing a crown of olive leaves, which indicates a royal personage, and the face is similar to ones stamped on many of the coins which have been found in the area."

"How long have you been interested in antiquities, Miss DeCamp?" Portia asked, noting with pleasure that several other guests were glancing their way with obvious interest. If she could just keep his lordship talking, she was certain it would encourage others to approach him.

"Oh, for several years," the other woman confessed with a soft laugh. "It was an interest of my grandfather's, and when he died he willed his collection to me."

"I also collect Roman coins and the like," Connor said, his voice losing some of its petulant edge. "I could show them to you later, if you would like?"

"What a marvelous idea!" Portia said before Miss DeCamp could speak. "And I am sure Mr. Pelligrew should also enjoy seeing them as well. Would you not, sir?" She turned to the dark-

haired Corinthian who had strolled over to join
them.

"As a matter of fact, I would," he agreed, tilting his head to one side and giving Connor a
teasing look. "Had no idea you were interested
in such things, old fellow," he drawled, hazel
eyes dancing with laughter. "To hear McLean
tell it, your interests are limited to sheep and
oats!"

"Ha, do not mention that scoundrel to me,"
Connor grumbled, still piqued by what he regarded as his friend's betrayal. "The wretch assured me he would be here, but at the last minute
he sent his regrets. Coward."

"His elder brother ordered him home to Buck-
inghamshire, and poor Keegan had no choice but
to comply." Mr. Pelligrew defended their mutual
friend with an indifferent shrug of his shoulders.
"Such is the fate of a younger brother, forever at
the beck and call of the true son and heir."

There was an uncomfortable silence, but fortunately for all, the Misses Darlington, emboldened
by the sight of the earl conversing with Miss De-
Camp, drifted over, and the conversation soon
turned to the topic of the London Season. The eldest Darlington girl had made her bows the year
before, and she was eager to flaunt her many suc-
cesses in her sisters' pretty faces.

Once she was certain the earl seemed comfortable, Portia drifted away. She checked on the
refreshments, and then joined the countess. She
found the older woman holding court in a corner
of the drawing room, enjoying a comfortable coze
with several other ladies. Portia recognized the
squire's and the vicar's wives, and after murmur-
ing a polite greeting she took a chair beside Lady
Eliza.

"Well, things certainly seem to be going well,

don't they?" the countess said, raising her teacup to Portia in a mock salute. "Congratulations, my dear, you have done the impossible. I never thought I should live to see that stiff-necked son of mine actually unbending enough to enjoy himself!"

"His lordship needed only a little encouragement, my lady," Portia replied modestly, although she was rather pleased with herself. The earl was now moving from group to group, and even if he was not gregarious, at least he no longer resembled one of those Roman statutes he seemed to find so fascinating.

"Who was that young lady you introduced to Doncaster?" Mrs. Hampson, the squire's practical wife, wanted to know, casting Miss DeCamp a speculative look. "She's a pretty little thing."

"Miss Felicity DeCamp," another lady answered, popping another biscuit in her mouth as she dispensed gossip. "Only daughter of a well-to-do farmer from Bath. Her paternal grandfather was the Marquess of Cromford, and her mother is the Brextons' cousin. She has two thousand per year, her own maid who travels with her, and she is rumored to be something of a bluestocking."

"Cromford's granddaughter, eh?" Lady Eliza examined Miss DeCamp with considerably more interest. "I was always rather fond of the old fellow; knew his way about horses and had more good sense than a marquess has a right to."

"You do not mean to consider her as a suitable wife for Doncaster?" Mrs. Crowell, the vicar's plump wife, protested, looking properly shocked. "My dear lady, it would never do!"

"And why no?" Lady Eliza demanded, scowling at the woman. "Two thousand per annum may not be a great deal, but as Doncaster is not hanging out for a fortune, it will do quite nicely. And she *is* a pretty little thing, isn't she? She would look stunning in the Doncaster pearls."

"It was not Miss DeCamp's fortune I was thinking of, Lady Doncaster," Mrs. Crowell said, obviously aware she had overstepped the bounds and eager to make amends. "It is just . . . well . . . I have spoken to her after services, and she is somewhat timid. Surely you would desire a wife with a bit of backbone for your son. He can be rather . . . er . . . that is to say . . ." Her face grew red as she stammered to a halt. Then she raised her cup to her lips for a noisy sip. "My, this is delicious tea! I believe I detect just a touch of Darjeeling in the blend."

For a moment Portia feared Lady Eliza would take up the cudgels on her son's behalf, but in the end she managed a brittle smile. "You are quite right, Fanny. What a clever tongue you have, to be sure."

Mrs. Crowell's face grew even redder, and the other ladies studiously addressed themselves to other topics. Portia listened half-attentively, dutifully contributing to the conversation even as her gaze kept returning to the earl. He was standing in front of the fireplace, gravely conversing with Lydia Brexton, and the sight of him made the breath catch in her throat. He really was a handsome man, she thought, admiring his rugged profile with what she assured herself was cool detachment.

Dressed in his stylish new jacket and elegant cravat, his dark hair cut to a fashionable length, he looked far different than the dark and dangerous man she had encountered in her bedchamber at the Red Dove. Oh, he was every bit as overwhelming, she acknowledged with a slight smile, noting the way he bowed over his lovely companion's hand, but now he didn't seem nearly so reserved. In fact, she mused, he seemed almost approachable. Perhaps there was some hope for the countess's plans after all.

Even as this optimistic thought was forming, she saw an odd look flash across his face. He straightened as if in pain, and took a hesitant step backwards, his face hardening into a mask of ice. Miss Brexton must have sensed something was amiss, for she gave him an apprehensive glance. The expression on his face had her stumbling back, and even as Portia looked on in horror, she picked up her skirts and fled to the other side of the room.

Portia was at his side in a thrice, praying no one else had noticed the little drama. "I cannot believe you!" she raged in a low, tight voice. "I leave you alone for a quarter hour, and you are back to your old tricks! What did you say to Miss Brexton to send her fleeing like that?"

His green eyes flashed with fury, but his posture remained rigid. "I said nothing amiss to the young lady. If she took flight, it has nothing to do with me."

"Oh, don't be so stuffy!" Portia grumbled, so incensed she forgot her manners. "And for heaven's sake, will you relax? You look like one of Madame Tussaud's wax figures standing there! Go over to Mrs. Darlington, and pay her your respects."

"I cannot."

She blinked at his blunt response. "What do you mean you can't?" she demanded. "She is sitting right over there!"

"I can see that, but that doesn't change the fact I cannot leave this corner."

"But why?" Portia was so vexed she could have shrieked.

He turned to her with a look that could have frozen fire. "Because, madam," he said through clenched teeth, "I have just split my breeches."

8

Portia could not believe her ears. Her first response was to laugh, but one look at the earl's face persuaded her this would not be wise. However humorous she might find the situation, it was obvious he did not share her amusement.

"What happened?" she asked, biting her lip.

The earl kept his gaze fixed on the opposite wall. "I told that fool of a valet the blasted things were too tight," he said, his cheeks reddening with mortification, "but he insisted 'twas all the fashion."

"And so it is," Portia agreed, her jaw aching as she fought a smile. "However, it might be best if we get you out of here so that you can change into a less ... er ... fashionable pair."

He flashed her a suspicious look. "Are you laughing at me?" he demanded, clearly outraged.

"I am trying very hard not to," she admitted, unfurling her painted silk fan to hide her grin. "Hush now, and let me think."

She pondered the matter for several seconds, trying to think of some logical, dignified way out of the contretemps, but not a single solution would come to mind. What *did* come to mind was a vague memory of a childhood scrape, and she frowned as she struggled to recall the details.

Her papa's sister had been visiting, she remembered, and she'd invited several of the neighboring ladies over for tea. Portia had begged and pleaded, and she'd finally been granted permission to attend on the condition that she behave herself. All had gone well until the small snake she had tucked in her apron pocket escaped, and crawled across the toes of the squire's wife's shoes. The good lady had responded with a screech that had rattled the windowpanes, and the rest of the ladies had rushed screaming from the sitting room. Her aunt had left the following morning, vowing never to return, and she'd spent the rest of the month in her room as punishment.

The memory of that afternoon made her chuckle, but it also made her think. What if a snake were to get loose in this room? she wondered, a plan beginning to form in her mind. The ladies would shriek, the gentlemen would shout, and in the ensuing confusion his lordship could slip quietly from the room, change his clothes, and return before anyone was the wiser. And in the event someone should remark upon his absence, he could always claim he'd gone off to get a gun to dispatch the creature.

Yes, she thought excitedly, *it could work*. It . . . No, her rational mind suddenly admonished. The very notion was childish. Ridiculous. It was certain to cause a scandal, and what was more she didn't even have a snake, and she could hardly leave the room to go in search of one.

"Why are you just standing there like a moonling?" the earl demanded impatiently, his dark brows meeting over his nose as he glowered at her. "Do something!"

Portia sent him an annoyed look. She could sympathize with him up to a point, but that didn't mean she was willing to let him treat her in so high-handed a manner. "I am endeavoring to think of a solution to your difficulty, my lord," she informed him loftily, "but the only idea I have come up with is certain to cause a dreadful scene."

"It couldn't possibly cause as big a scene as I shall cause if I am forced to leave this corner," he returned grimly, looking desperate.

Portia glanced from him to the crowded room. "If your lordship is certain . . ."

"So long as it doesn't involve setting fire to the drapes, you may do whatever you please!" he interrupted, steeling himself as if for battle. "Just be quick about it!"

"Very well, sir, if that is what you wish." She left his side and made her way over to where the Misses Darlington were holding court. She bent over the eldest girl and whispered in her ear.

"A snake!" the younger woman exclaimed, leaping to her feet and regarding Portia with horror. "In here?"

"Just a tiny one," Portia assured her with a placating smile. "I'm not certain how it slithered under the settee but—"

The rest of her apology was lost in the cacophony of screams that followed. The settee was knocked back as the three young ladies leaped to their feet, their skirts raised to show a shocking amount of ankle as they fled screaming from the room. Their mama, seeing her daughters comporting themselves with such a singular lack of decorum but not knowing the cause, also began to shriek, clasping her hand to her bosom and affecting a most dramatic swoon. Several other ladies followed suit, and within seconds what had been a quiet tea party disintegrated into a small riot, the subject of which would provide tidbits of gossip for many years to come.

* * *

"I have never been so embarrassed in all my life!" Lady Eliza moaned some thirty minutes later, her head resting on her hand as she gazed about the wrecked drawing room. "Really, Portia, how *could* you?"

"But, my lady, it is as I have already explained!" Portia cried, genuinely hurt by the countess's criticism. "The situation was a desperate one, and I had to do something! What other choice did I have?"

"But a snake?" the countess wailed. "It will be weeks before I will be able to lift my head in church, and I shall consider myself fortunate if any of my neighbors deign to notice me again. We are ruined!"

The earl, who had been leaning against the mantelpiece, straightened, his expression darkening as he studied his mother. "Come, Mama, surely you are painting the situation blacker than it really is," he said coolly. "No one was hurt, and as for anyone snubbing you, I sincerely doubt that is a possibility. You are the Countess of Doncaster, and I shall have the head of any man who dares to slight you."

"Imbecile!" the countess snapped, transferring her displeasure to her son. "As if it was the men I needed to worry about!"

"If anyone runs the risk of being snubbed, it is me. I was the one who instigated the melee, after all," Portia intervened quietly, hating that she should be the cause of a rift between mother and son. It reminded her too much of the quarrels with her papa, and she ached with guilt.

"Nonsense!" Lord Doncaster gave her a stern look. "No one in this house will be snubbed by anyone. I shall see to that."

"How?" Lady Eliza demanded.

"I shall ride into town tomorrow and pay a call

on the vicar," he answered decisively, ignoring her stunned expression. "I shall also call on the squire and the Darlingtons, just to be sure Mrs. Darlington has recovered from her fit of the vapors."

"*You* will visit our neighbors?" the countess repeated in disbelief. "To pay social calls?"

"I have been known to leave the estate on occasion, ma'am," he said in a cold voice, his eyes flicking to Portia. "Despite what some may say, I am hardly a hermit. I will ride out first thing tomorrow."

The countess opened her mouth as if to say something, and then closed it again. "An excellent plan," she said at last, nodding in approval. "Only mind you do not ride out too early. Although this is York, the Darlingtons will doubtlessly keep town hours. It will be best if you put off your call until after luncheon. Naturally Miss Haverall shall accompany you."

Portia gave a surprised start. "Me, my lady?"

"Well, I cannot go with him," the countess said with obvious impatience, "and it would cause no end of speculation if he were to call upon a bevy of unmarried ladies without some kind of female to lend him countenance. Speaking of which, Gwynnen shall accompany you as well. As you are now a guest in our home, we must take every care that your reputation is protected."

It all sounded nonsensical to Portia, but she bowed to the countess's superior knowledge in such matters. "As you wish, Lady Doncaster," she said, deciding now was as good a time as any to stage a strategic retreat. She was still somewhat overset by the afternoon's events, and the thought of a warm bath and a few hours' privacy in which to regain her equilibrium was sweetly tempting. Even though she knew it was cowardly, she rose to her feet and curtsied to both the countess and her brooding son.

"If you will pardon me, I believe I shall retire to my room for the evening," she said, keeping her face expressionless as she met the earl's watchful gaze. "What time would you like to leave tomorrow, my lord?"

He took so long in answering that Portia wondered if she should repeat the question. "Two o'clock will be fine," he said at last, his gaze thoughtful as he studied her. "In the meanwhile, I will send them notes so that they will expect us. I do not wish to arrive unannounced."

That made sense to Portia, and she murmured her agreement. She walked over to the door, and was surprised when the earl moved away from the fireplace to join her.

"I would like a word with you, if you do not mind," he said, opening the door with one hand, and cupping her elbow with the other. He guided her out into the hall, and after a quick glance about to make sure they were alone, he turned back to her.

"I haven't had a chance to thank you for your quick thinking," he said, his voice low as he took her hand in his. "I am not certain what I would have done had it not been for your . . . creative diversion shall we say. It was most effective."

"You did say I could do whatever I pleased so long as I did not set fire to the drapes," Portia reminded him, her heart racing at the feel of his warm hand cradling hers. She wasn't so green that this was the first time a gentleman had ever held her hand, but it was the first time she had enjoyed it so much. The realization shocked her, and she ruthlessly suppressed it.

The edges of his mouth curved in a wry smile. "So I did," he agreed with a low chuckle. "Now I wonder if a small fire would have proven less dangerous than an imaginary snake. I have never seen a room emptied quite so quickly. It is a miracle no one was injured in the rush for the door."

Despite her conflicting emotions, Portia was unable to hold back a slight smile. "I did see the vicar's wife moving with amazing dexterity," she informed him, eyes sparkling. "And the vicar himself managed to push his way past several of the younger ladies to be among the first out of the room. I was shocked."

"Yes, one would think a man of God would have more courage when confronting a serpent," he agreed, raising her hand to his lips for a brief kiss. "My thanks once again, Portia," he said, his voice unexpectedly grave as he used her given name for the first time. "I am in your debt."

Portia knew she should respond, but for the life of her, the words would not come. A dozen different thoughts and emotions whirled about in her head, and she could not even begin to sort them all out. Finally her pride asserted itself, and she even managed a polite smile as she tugged her hand free from his.

"You are most welcome, sir," she said, her voice coolly polite as she stepped back. "Now if you will excuse me, I really am tired. Good evening, my lord. I shall see you tomorrow afternoon." With that she turned and hurried away, unaware of the dark-green eyes that followed her flight.

Connor spent the next morning tending to his estate, and brooding over the coming afternoon. He was already regretting his impulsive promise to visit the Darlingtons, but having given his word, he could think of no honorable way to cry off. He was well and truly trapped, and the feeling of helplessness added to his growing resentment.

This was all Portia's fault, he decided, grunting
as he heaved a bale of hay down from the loft. If
she hadn't insisted upon rigging him out like a
London dandy, none of this would have happened. He had been content with the way things
were, and he could see no reason why he should
change to accommodate her.

Less than a moment after these unworthy
thoughts popped into his head, he was renouncing
them with an angry mutter. If anyone was to
blame for yesterday's farce, it was himself. He
should have known better than to think the Ox
could make it through even so prosaic an event as
a tea party without making an ass out of himself.
Perhaps that would have made a more fitting
nickname, he mused, tossing another bale over the
edge, although he supposed it lacked the panache
of "the Ox from Oxford."

" 'Ere now! Mind where ye be tossin' them
bales!" an indignant voice cried out, and Connor
glanced down to see the stable hand who had
been assisting him glowering up at him.

"Aye, I be down 'ere, me lord," the older man
retorted with a singular lack of respect, "although
ye liked to flatten me with that last bale!"

Connor was too accustomed to the man's sharp
tongue to take umbrage at such frank speech. "My
apologies, McNeil," he called down, wiping his
arm across his sweat-dampened forehead. "I fear I
wasn't as attentive as I should have been."

"Maybe we need to be tradin' places," the older
man suggested with an aggrieved scowl. "A man
what can't keep 'is mind on 'is work oughtn't to
be tossin' 'ay down from a loft."

As this was patently true, Connor took no offense. He had worked long and hard to be accepted by his men, and he wasn't about to
jeopardize that by flying into the boughs because

of a well-deserved scold. He apologized once again and went back to work, this time taking greater care.

After tossing down the last bale, Connor climbed down and began raking out the stalls. The work was hard, but he took pleasure in it, easily losing himself in the backbreaking task. If only the rest of life was as simple as mucking out a stall, he thought, indulging in a rare philosophical moment. He could deal with the dirt and the sweat, but the intricacies of society often left him baffled.

He was mulling over the matter when something made him glance up. Miss Haverall was standing in the doorway, her gray eyes wide as they rested on his bare chest. He set his shovel to one side, and reached for the shirt he had discarded earlier.

"Good morning, ma'am," he said, pulling the rough cambric over his head, and doing his best to look nonchalant. "Is there something I can do for you?"

She swallowed nervously, her eyes wide as they rested on his hair-roughened chest. "I . . . Lady Eliza asked that I bring you back to the house," she stammered, her cheeks beginning to grow pink with embarrassment. "She is afraid you will be late if we do not hurry."

"That is very kind of Mother, but unnecessary. I was just about to stop for the day," Connor replied, grabbing his jacket from the hook by the door. He could tell that she was deeply shocked, but decided it was wisest to say nothing. If he apologized, it would draw attention to the fact that she had glimpsed him half-clothed, which would only add to her mortification.

They walked back toward the house in silence. Portia was slightly ahead of him, and if the stiff way she held herself was any indication, it was obvious she was doing her best to recover her composure. He decided he had remained silent long enough, and lengthened his stride until he was beside her.

"And how did you spend your morning, ma'am?" he asked in what he hoped was a casual manner. "I trust you and Mama have been keeping yourselves busy?"

"Indeed we have, sir," she replied, her gaze set firmly in front of her. "We have finished all of our correspondence, and are looking over menus for the next fortnight."

"I trust you remembered to tell Cook not to prepare any more oysters," Connor remarked, determined to set her at her ease. "I cannot imagine what made her serve them in the first place. She must know I can not abide shellfish."

"I will have a word with her," she replied, keeping her eyes fixed firmly ahead of her as she continued up the path.

Connor decided he'd had enough, and stopped walking. "Blast it, Portia," he exclaimed, reaching out to snag her arm and pull her to a halt. "Will you stop acting so missish? I am sorry you saw me without my shirt, but I always take it off when I am working with the hay. How was I to know you would be in the stables!"

To his annoyance she took instant umbrage to his words. "I am not behaving missishly!" she denied, jerking her elbow free and glaring at him through narrowed eyes. "And as for my being in the stables, I told you your mother sent me to fetch you!"

"I don't care why you were there, I am only saying that I didn't mean to shock you," Connor said through clenched teeth, determined not to lose his

temper. He couldn't remember the last time a female had affected him so strongly, but he did
know he was growing weary of it.

"I wasn't shocked ... precisely," she replied, re-
laxing enough to offer him a tentative smile.
"Now, let us say no more of the matter. I am sure
you will agree the less said, the better."

Connor did not agree, but as a gentleman he
must do as she requested. They resumed walking,
and this time it was Portia who broke the silence.

"I must say I am looking forward to seeing a bit
more of the countryside today," she remarked as
they skirted a hay cart. "Is it as lovely as they say
it is?"

"Better," he said, feeling a twinge of guilt as he
realized he had been derelict in his duties as a
host. It should have occurred to him that Portia
would want the chance to explore the neighborhood. "Perhaps if we have time I shall drive you
into York so that you can see the minster," he offered, anxious to correct his negligence. "It is
huge, and, to my mind, every bit as grand as the
cathedral in Canterbury."

"Spoken like a true Yorkshireman, my lord,"
Portia said, and Connor relaxed at the teasing note
in her voice. He'd grown accustomed to speaking
freely with her, and it troubled him to have the
slightest enmity between them.

"Perhaps that is because we have so much to be
proud of," he suggested, noting with regret that
they had almost reached the house. He was enjoying their talk so much, he would not have objected
if they kept walking for the rest of the afternoon.
Ah, well, he consoled himself with a sigh, there
was still the drive to the Darlingtons'. The thought
made him smile, and suddenly he could not wait
for the afternoon to arrive.

* * *

Portia and Connor, accompanied by Gwynnen, set out for their journey in high spirits. The Darlingtons' home lay between Hawkshurst and York, and they reached it in less than half an hour. Portia was not surprised to find the entire family assembled in the drawing room awaiting their arrival. Mrs. Darlington had indeed recovered her nerves, and if her greeting to Portia was less cordial than it might have been, there was no faulting the warmth with which she welcomed the earl.

"*Dear* Lord Doncaster," she fairly gushed, thrusting out her hand to Connor so that he might kiss it. "Such a delight to see you again! And pray how is your mama this morning?"

"She is well, ma'am," Connor answered, and the twinkle in his eyes told Portia he was doing his best not to laugh at the lady's effusive greeting. "I shall be certain to mention that you asked after her."

"I was going to call upon her myself," Mrs. Darlington continued in her ebullient manner, "for I have so many questions to ask her. There is the matter of clothes to be considered, of course, and the parties to be planned. My, but we shall be gay this summer! My girls and I are quite looking forward to it, aren't we, lambkins?" She turned a fond maternal eye on her three daughters sitting in blonde perfection on the opposite settee.

"Yes, Mama," they chorused, fluttering their lashes at Connor and sending him dimpled smiles.

"Naturally, one may hope the house will be cleansed of reptiles before the festivities begin," Mrs. Darlington added with a sniff, addressing Portia for the first time.

Portia, who had begun to grow bored with the pedestrian nature of the conversation, brightened at the display of poor manners. "Oh, there is no need to fear on that account, Mrs. Darlington," she answered with a dimpled smile of her own. "I have had a new cage built for Prinny, and I assure you he shan't escape again. The poor thing was quite upset by all the excitement, you know. I was hours calming him down."

A stunned silence filled the room as the Darlingtons exchanged horrified looks. "You . . . you have a pet snake?" Mrs. Darlington asked, her voice shaking so much Portia wondered if they were about to be treated to another dramatic swoon.

"Just a tiny garden snake," Portia said, enjoying herself more than she had in months. "He is very colorful, however, which is why I named him for the Regent. His lordship gave him to me," she added, a sudden imp of mischief making her include the earl in her deception. To her delight he picked up the reins at once, his expression solemn as he took the cup of tea that a visibly shaken Mrs. Darlington offered him.

"Yes, I read a fascinating article in one of my farming journals suggesting that snakes are far better than cats at keeping the mice down," he said coolly, raising his cup to his lips. "It worked astonishingly well in the stables, and so I decided to try them in the house. We haven't heard a single squeak or rustle in weeks."

"Snakes, eh?" Mr. Darlington spoke for the first time, the expression on his florid face thoughtful. "Worth a try, I suppose. Only last week Cook was complaining about the vermin in our larder—"

"Edgar!"

"Papa!"

A chorus of outraged female voices drowned out the rest of Mr. Darlington's observation. The rest of the visit was conducted with stiff civility, and at the end the Darlingtons seemed almost relieved to be shed of their highborn guest and his outrageous companion.

"You are a menace," Connor remarked with a chuckle as they rolled down the road toward their next stop. He had eschewed his elaborate carriage and its driver in favor of his light phaeton, and he took obvious pleasure in handling the ribbons himself.

"Snakes in the house," he continued, shaking his head in mock despair. "I don't know what compelled me to support such an outrageous clanker. Now it will be all over the neighborhood that Hawkshurst is overrun with vipers."

"Better to be overrun with snakes than to lay claim to mice in the larder," Portia retorted with a smug laugh, reveling in the havoc she had caused. After so many months of determinedly minding her every word, it felt wonderful to be her old, contentious self again. Mayhap she would allow herself an outrageous remark or two a week, she decided with a secretive smile. She had forgotten how much fun it could be.

"That is true," Connor agreed with a grin. "Did you see the expression on our hostess's face when her husband blurted out his artless confession? I daresay she read him a thundering scold before the door had even closed behind us."

"I am sure she must have," Portia said, recalling the knife-edged glares the other lady had cast her hapless mate. "I also noted no one took any of the cakes and sandwiches when they were offered. Ah, well." She tilted her head to one side and fluttered her lashes at him in perfect imitation of the Misses Darlington. "Perhaps the mice will enjoy them."

Their visit to the vicar's was less eventful, as Portia remained on her best behavior. After listening to a long-winded lecture about the sacred duties of a host and hostess, and choking down a cup of weak tea, they were allowed to go on their way. The vicar also extracted a promise from Connor to attend services on a more regular basis, and as they made their way to the squire's house, Portia teased him about his dereliction to his immortal soul.

"Never say I have been residing with an atheist," she teased, laughing at the mulish expression on his face. "For shame, sir, have you no regard at all for the proprieties?"

"I am not an atheist," he denied, tearing his gaze from the road to send her an indignant scowl. "And you are a fine one to talk about disregarding the proprieties, ma'am. You haven't behaved with an iota of propriety since the moment we met."

"Ha! And you have the nerve to say *I* tell clankers!" Portia laughed, too high-spirited to take offense at the accusation. She turned to Gwynnen with a wheedling smile.

"Come, Gwynnen," she coaxed playfully, "tell this blackened sinner that my behavior has remained above reproach. I have been the very model of feminine decorum, have I not?"

"Wouldn't go so far as to say that," the taciturn maid answered in her usual blunt manner. "But you haven't tried to dash out his lordship's brains again, I'll grant you that."

"There, you see?" Portia affected a prim expression, hands folded and gaze demurely lowered. "I have been the very soul of sensibility and moderation. You would do well to follow my pattern, sir."

Connor gave a reluctant chuckle. "Were I to do that, ma'am, my reputation would be even worse than it is," he said, and from this tone Portia could see he did not seem so bitter. "Now mind you keep a lock on that outrageous tongue of yours for the rest of the day. I would as lief not alienate all of my neighbors in a single afternoon."

Two days later, Portia was sitting in her room going over the last of her lists. The guests had all written back with their acceptances, and in less than a sennight Hawkshurst would be filled to overflowing with people. The countess had promised to see that additional staff would be hired, and that the proper foods would be brought in from London, and left the planning of events to Portia's discretion.

All was going as well as she could have hoped, but instead of satisfaction in a job well done, Portia felt only shame. The countess was still insisting upon secrecy, and that meant his lordship remained ignorant of the coming invasion. She hated the thought of breaking her promise to her ladyship, but she hated more the thought of deceiving the earl. He had a right to know what was going on in his own house, she thought, and decided it was time to inform him of what was about to happen. She knew the countess would be angry, but that was a risk she was prepared to take.

Once she had reached that decision, the rest of the afternoon passed swiftly. In addition to the many teas, soiress, and card games, the house party would end in a grand ball, and in a flash of inspiration Portia had decided to make it a costume ball. She had never been to one, but they sounded like great fun, and she began sketching out various ideas for themes. The matter of costumes was another difficulty, and she decided to seek out the countess's advice. She was so preoccupied with the ball that she completely forgot to knock, but walked into Lady Eliza's rooms unannounced.

"My lady, I was wondering if I might have a word with you," she said, casually glancing up. "I have an idea for—" Her voice broke off, and she stared at the countess in disbelief. "Lady Doncaster!" she gasped, the list fluttering from her hand. "You can walk!"

9

Lady Eliza turned around, her expression first startled and then resigned as she saw Portia standing in the doorway. "Oh, dear," she said, sighing as she set down the porcelain figurine she had been holding, "it appears you have found me out."

"I . . . I do not understand," Portia stammered, advancing into the room, unable to take her gaze off the amazing sight of the countess standing in front of the fireplace. "Connor . . . Lord Doncaster told me you had been paralyzed in a fall!"

"And so I was," Lady Eliza replied calmly, crossing the room to take Portia's hand. "If you will give me a moment, I promise I will explain everything."

"But you can walk!" Portia said, still not believing the evidence of her own eyes. Her shock was gradually fading, and in its place was a rising sense of indignation. She remembered the expression on the earl's face, the pain in his voice when he had first told her of his mother's condition, and she shook her head.

"My lady, how could you do this to your own son?" she chided, appalled that anyone could be so cruel. "Do you not know what it does to him to see you in that chair, believing himself responsible for your being there?"

Tears gathered in the countess's eyes, but she did not let them fall. "It sounds heartless, I know," she admitted in a quiet voice, "but I assure you I do have a very good reason for what I have done. Let us sit down, and I will tell you the whole of it."

Portia allowed herself to be guided over to the settee, her gaze fixed on the countess as they took their seats. Lady Eliza settled her skirts about her, her eyes lowered to her lap as she began speaking.

"When the accident first happened, I truly was paralyzed," she began without preamble. "I could not move my legs, and the doctors could offer us no hope. I thought I would spend the rest of my days trapped in that blasted chair. And then gradually, feeling began to return. I was afraid to believe it at first, but when it was obvious I was recovering, I cannot tell you how thankful and relieved I was."

"I can understand that," Portia said gently, reaching out to cover the countess's hand with her own, "but why did you fail to share the joyous news with your son? You must have known he would want to know."

Lady Eliza gave a jerky nod. "I... I knew he held himself to blame for what happened," she said in a low voice, raising her eyes to meet Portia's gaze, "and I was going to tell him I could walk again, but... Oh, this is going to sound so dreadful!"

"What is going to sound so dreadful?" Portia asked as the countess covered her face with her hands.

"But I realized that if Connor thought I was still injured, he would be more amenable to getting married," Lady Eliza concluded in the tone of one confessing to a terrible crime. She dropped her hands and met Portia's startled gaze. "You think I'm terrible, don't you?" she asked miserably.

"I don't know what I think," Portia answered, too amazed to be anything other than completely candid. She had never heard of such a calculating act in her life, and the worst part was, even as part of her was horrified by the countess's actions, the other part was applauding her ingenuity.

"You think I'm dreadful," Lady Eliza sniffed, her green eyes filling with tears, "and I cannot say that I blame you. You are so honest and forthright, I know you would never dream of doing anything so conniving."

"I would not say that," Portia mumbled, recalling the times she had feigned illness to get out of some task her father had set for her.

"I never meant for the deception to go on so long," Lady Eliza continued in an unhappy voice. "But the weeks became months, and the months somehow turned into a year, and I could not think of any way to end the charade. I was trapped in that Bath chair by my own duplicity, as surely as if I'd been put there by the fall. I was at my wit's end until you came."

"Me?" Portia was startled by the countess's remark. "My lady, what are you saying? What has my coming here to do with anything?"

"Because for the first time since the accident, that stubborn son of mine has finally agreed to participate in the social round. Oh, I know it was but one afternoon," she added when Portia would have spoken, "and there's no denying it ended in disaster, but the important thing is that he participated. Until I saw him laughing and talking with Miss DeCamp, I was beginning to fear he would never marry."

Portia remembered the easy way the earl had conversed with Miss DeCamp, and an unfamiliar pain pierced her heart. "That is all very well, my lady," she said quickly, her gruff tone hiding her confusion, "but what do you propose we do now? You cannot mean to continue this charade indefinitely."

The countess gave her a hopeful look. "Well, actually . . ."

"No," Portia interrupted, shaking her head. "I cannot allow you to keep deceiving his lordship. It is too cruel."

"But I cannot simply walk up to him and admit the truth!" Lady Eliza protested in alarm. "It would ruin everything, and he would never forgive me!"

As Portia could well imagine the earl's response, she sympathized with the countess's reluctance to confess all. Still, she couldn't allow him to continue blaming himself for something which wasn't even his fault. She tapped her foot thoughtfully, her brows gathering in a frown as she tried to think of a way out of their predicament.

"A month," she said at last, fixing the countess with a stern gaze. "I will give you a month to 'recover,' or I shall be forced to tell Lord Doncaster the truth."

Lady Eliza looked as if she would have liked to argue the point, but at the expression on Portia's face, she gave a defeated sigh. "Very well," she said, "if you are going to be that way about it. I will do as you insist."

Portia refused to feel guilty. "Good," she said coolly. "You may begin by using a regular wheelchair. It will grant you more mobility, and help convince his lordship that your recovery is gradual, and therefore genuine."

"Do you mean I shan't be allowed to miraculously walk?" Lady Eliza asked sweetly. "What a pity. It would have given our houseguests something to gossip about for years to come."

"And there is another thing," Portia said, ignoring the other lady's sarcasm. "I have never approved of your insistence that we not tell his lordship about our houseguests. I want your permission to apprise him of our plans."

"Tell him!" Lady Eliza protested indignantly. "But—"

"It's either that, or telling him his mama has been deceiving him all this time," Portia said calmly, folding her arms across her chest and meeting the countess's gaze. "It is your choice."

Lady Eliza's bottom lip thrust forward in a mutinous pout. "As you wish," she said petulantly, clearly put out. "But I must say I am disappointed in you. I thought you were my friend."

"I am," Portia said, "but I also count myself your son's friend, and friends do not deceive each other."

"Do they not?" Lady Eliza gave her a crafty smile. "If you say so, my dear, if you say so."

After returning to her own rooms, Portia found she was too restless to resume her work. The sun streaming through the mullioned windows was a sweet temptation, and she decided to go out for a ride. She rang for her maid, and thirty minutes later she was on the mare the earl had selected for her, the warm wind caressing her cheeks as she rode over a rocky rise. She reined in her mount with a joyous laugh, her heart filled with pleasure as she gazed at the pastoral scene spread out beneath her.

Well-fed sheep grazed in green fields neatly enclosed by gray stone fences, and a clear brook tumbled over moss-covered rocks. In the distance she could see the ruins the earl had shown her on their first ride, and on impulse, she decided to ride over for a closer look. She'd just started down the steep hill when she heard someone call her name. She turned her head and saw Connor riding toward her.

"Good afternoon, Miss Haverall!" he called out, his black stallion rearing as he reined to a halt beside her. "A lovely day, is it not?"

"Very lovely, sir. I was hard at work in my rooms when I happened to look out the window. When I saw all this glorious sunshine, I couldn't remain indoors another moment longer." If any of those haughty London ladies could see him now, she thought, they would rue their cruel words.

His green eyes sparkled at her reply. "Deserted your post, have you?" he drawled, his lips curving in a teasing smile as he leaned over his saddle.

Portia's heart gave an alarming skip at the intimacy of that smile. "So it would appear, my lord," she said, unable to resist teasing him in return. "Will you have me shot?"

"That is the usual punishment for desertion," he reminded her, "but as I have also deserted my post, I suppose I shall have to be lenient."

She fluttered her lashes at him. "Your lordship is too kind," she said, her tone so sweet that he laughed in response.

As if by unspoken agreement they both nudged their horses forward, resuming their ride in silence. "Where were you headed when I first saw you?" he asked after they'd ridden some distance. "Anywhere in particular, or were you just letting your horse take you where she will?"

"I was on my way to the old ruins," Portia answered, deciding now was as good a time as any to inform him of the impending invasion. "I thought our guests would enjoy visiting it, and I wanted to see if I could find it on my own."

As she expected, he was quick to seize upon her words. "What guests?" he demanded.

"The ones who will be arriving next week," she replied as nonchalantly as she could. "You *did* say your mother could invite some friends to stay with her," she added when he frowned at her.

"I am well aware of that," he returned, the mouth that had been smiling only moments before now set in a grim line. "But I had no idea matters had progressed so far." His gaze shot to her face. "How long have you and mother been planning this?"

"Since our conversation the day Lady Alterwaithe's letter arrived," Portia replied, wondering why the duplicitous nature she had once abhorred in herself should choose this moment to desert her. In the past she would have lied and schemed without a twinge, telling herself it was for the earl's own good. Now it was all she could do not to throw herself at his feet, and beg for his forgiveness.

"And you never thought to inform me of these plans?" he asked, pulling his horse to a halt. "You and my mother invited guests to my home without so much as a by-your-leave?"

The sharp edge in his voice brought Portia's chin up. As guilty as she might feel for deceiving him, she wasn't about to let him question her like a common criminal. "You had already given your leave, sir," she reminded him in a clipped voice. "And as for keeping you *informed*, we simply saw no need to bother you with such trifling matters as what food to serve, and what room to assign to what guest. However, if you prefer, I should be more than happy to turn the entire thing over to your capable hands. I am sure you will be able to do a much better job. Good day." She would have ridden off, but he anticipated her move and reached out to grab her horse's reins.

Their eyes met, and for the briefest moment Portia felt a small frisson of alarm. For the first time since their unorthodox meeting, Connor's size seemed threatening. But even as her heart was beginning to race, he released the bridle and leaned back in his saddle.

"You ought to do something about that temper of yours, Miss Haverall," he advised, his expression remote. "It is regrettably short."

Despite that her palms were still damp with fear, Portia refused to cower before him. "As is yours, my lord," she returned, her tone matching his for coolness.

He regarded her for a long moment. "Perhaps," he agreed at last, the ice melting in his jewel-colored eyes. "But as I have already explained, I am said to resemble my late grandfather, the Beast of Hawkshurst Hall."

Portia remembered the conversation, and the portrait of the formidable Fourth Earl of Doncaster. "Then you admit your actions were beastly?" she challenged, praying he would take the words as the jest she intended, and not fly into the boughs.

To her relief he gave a reluctant smile. "I ought to have known better than to cross verbal swords with you," he said with a soft chuckle. "You have proven yourself a past master of the game. Very well, then, when may we expect the invading hordes to descend upon us?"

His easy acceptance of the prospect of guests made Portia blink, and it took her a few seconds to recover enough to answer him. "The first will be arriving at the end of next week," she said, mentally reviewing the preparations. "And the rest will arrive the week after that."

"The rest? How many guests are you expecting?"

"Fifteen, not counting servants and the like."

"Fifteen?" Connor frowned in displeasure at the thought of his domain being overrun by so many strangers. "Who are they?"

Portia dutifully rattled off everyone on the guest list she said she could remember, and by the time she was finished Connor was feeling positively grim.

"I see," he said, as they continued riding. "So that is why she is doing it."

"Why who is doing what?" Portia asked.

Connor wasn't fooled by her feigned innocence. "Come now, Portia," he reproved with a weary laugh, "it ill becomes you to play the fool. You know perfectly well that my mother engineered this house party for the sole purpose of throwing me together with prospective brides."

"Well, of course she did!" Portia replied. "You told me weeks ago that she was anxious to see you wed. What else would you have the poor lady do?"

Her sharp retort surprised Connor. "Allow me to pick my own bride in my own time?" he suggested hopefully.

She shot him a scornful look. "Don't be ridiculous," she said with a sniff. "If it was left to men to decide such things, marriage as an institution would have expired years ago! You are over thirty, and it is past time you were taking a wife."

Connor thought of the lady to whom he had once offered his title, and her brutal rejection of that title and him. The memory had long since lost its sting, but he was vaguely surprised to realize that in addition to indifference, he also felt a strong sense of relief. The realization was decid-

edly disconcerting, and to hide his confusion he
began to tease his companion.

"And what of you, Portia?" he asked, deliberately using her Christian name to provoke her.
"You are in your late twenties; should *you* not be
taking a husband?"

"I am but twenty-five!" she retorted. "And as
for my taking a husband, why ever should I want
to do such a harebrained thing? Husbands are
nothing but bother to an intelligent female like me,
and even if I was so foolish as to desire one of the
tiresome creatures, what man would want to leg-
shackle himself to a plain-faced, managing bluestocking?"

Her vehemence made Connor stare. "You are
not in the least plain!" he exclaimed, angry that
she should describe herself in such insulting
terms.

"We are not talking about me," Portia snapped,
annoyed with herself for the revealing remark.
"We are talking about *you*. You are the Earl of
Doncaster, and it is your duty to marry and pro-
duce an heir. If your mother must resort to mach-
inations to see you wed, it is only because you
have been so behindhand in seeing to the matter
yourself."

They had reached the ruins, and Connor dis-
mounted in silence before turning to help Portia.
His gloved hands easily encompassed her waist,
and he lifted her down as if she weighed no more
than a child. Without speaking, he led her over to
the ruined chapel, and while Portia seated herself
on one of the fallen stones, he rested one booted
foot beside her, his expression bleak as he gazed
off at the horizon.

"I know I should take a wife," he said in a
heavy tone, "and better than you, I know where

my duty lies. But knowing one's duty and acting on it are not always as easy as they sound."

Portia saw the anguish on his face, and wondered if she should tell him she was aware of his past. She debated the matter for several seconds before reaching her decision.

"Your mother told me about Lady Duxford," she said, biting her lip when she saw him flinch, "and while it is regrettable your first love should have proved to be a heartless flirt, you must not allow her memory to dictate the rest of your life. There are many other ladies in the world who would consider it a great honor to be your wife."

"Are there?" His lips twisted in a bitter smile. "If there are, these mysterious ladies have taken their own sweet time in making their presence known."

Portia's first instinct was to comfort him, but she knew he would regard her actions as being pity, motivated by an emotion he would most certainly abhor. "Well, what can you expect, keeping yourself hidden on your estate?" she asked in a gruff voice. "Your mama tells me it has been years since you last attended so much as an assembly."

That drew his gaze to her. "Did she tell you what happened the last time I attended one of those wretched things?" he asked in a tight voice. "I asked two ladies to stand up with me for a quadrille. *Two*, and they both fainted."

Portia thought of how intimidating he could be, but decided that did not excuse the silly chits. "Well then, all I can say is that you obviously asked the wrong ladies," she continued in the same curt manner. "Can you imagine either Miss DeCamp or myself behaving in such a singularly foolish manner?"

He dropped his arm and rose slowly to his full height, his expression shuttered as he stared down at her. "Are you saying that you would dance with me?" he challenged, holding her in his steady gaze.

"Of course I would," she said, thinking of all those years in Chipping Campden when she sat with the dowagers, sniffing in derision at the dancers even as she silently prayed to be asked.

"All right."

The non sequitur made her frown. "All right what?"

"All right," he repeated calmly, "I will attend the next assembly, but only on the condition that you attend, and that you dance with me."

Portia's jaw dropped, and had it not been for the expression on his face, she would have laughed outright. "But my lord," she began with a nervous laugh, "I am your mother's companion—"

"No," he interrupted, "you're not. You are our guest, and no one would think it odd if I were to ask you to dance; quite the opposite, in fact. I would look like the worst host in all of Christendom were I not to stand up with you."

Portia knew he was right, and that there would be even more scandal attached to his name if he slighted her in such a public way. "Yes, there is that, I suppose," she admitted reluctantly, "but I would still prefer that you ask one of the other ladies. Miss DeCamp, perhaps, or one of the Misses Darlington. And of course, once your mama's guests arrive, you will have any number of females to choose as your partner. I—" She broke off abruptly as a sudden thought occurred to her.

"You do dance?" she asked, bending a suspicious frown on him.

Connor clenched his fist at the querulous demand. "Yes, I dance," he replied in a cold voice.

"What of waltzing?"

He frowned. "What of it?"

She sighed heavily, wondering if he was being deliberately obtuse. "Do you waltz?" she asked, struggling for control.

"As it was not the fashion when I was in London, I fear I do not," Connor replied, as if hating to admit such a deficiency to her. "However, I doubt it will be much of a problem at the assembly. York is not London, and such wanton behavior is frowned upon. I would be surprised if the master of ceremonies would allow a single waltz, if that."

"Perhaps," Portia said, recalling how scandalized the locals were the first time the waltz was performed in Chipping Campden, "but your mother's guests will be slightly more cosmopolitan in their views, and they *will* expect the waltz to be played at the costume ball."

Connor wanted to ask what costume ball, but he decided the question could wait. Instead, a delightful scheme was forming in his mind. He crossed his arms and gave her a cool smile.

"Again, I see no great difficulty," he said, his voice consciously pitched to its most seductive level. "If you wish me to waltz, then you have only to teach me."

The riot of color that flooded Portia's face delighted Connor. "I cannot teach you to waltz!" she exclaimed, looking thoroughly vexed.

"Why not?" he asked, opening his eyes wide and feigning shock. "Are you saying that *you* do not waltz?"

"Of course I waltz!" she snapped. "That is to say, I have learned the dance, but I have never actually performed it."

He gave a pleased nod. "Then we shall learn from each other. When would you like to start?"

Portia opened her mouth to continue arguing,

but realized the wretch had outmaneuvered her. There was no way she could insist he learn to dance if she did not follow suit. "You are enjoying this, aren't you?" she accused, shooting him a sour look.

The grin he gave her was patently self-satisfied. "Not yet, my dear," he drawled, his green eyes dancing. "But I will."

Over the next few days Portia was kept busy as she rushed about making sure all was in readiness for the guests' arrival. The rooms were all cleaned and awaiting their occupants, and plans for the many entertainments were continuing apace. There were to be several picnics, excursions into York to visit the famous minster, and, of course, any number of card and dancing parties to keep their jaded guests from becoming bored.

After discussing the matter with the countess, she decided to hold the costume ball. They were seldom held these days, Lady Eliza told her, and that would make it the perfect cap for the house party. People would talk about it for months, and it would be the social event of the neighborhood. Hurried notes were sent out advising their guests of the need for a costume, and one of the footmen was sent into York to make sure costumes would be made available for those who did not bring their own.

The day before the first guest was to arrive, Portia was in the wine cellars completing one last inventory. She and the butler had already marked several bottles of port and brandy for use, but she wanted to make sure there would be some light wine and sherry available for the ladies. She was examining a bottle of Spanish sherry when she heard the earl calling out her name. She answered, and he came clattering noisily down the steps.

"There you are," he said, hands on his narrow hips as he glared down at her. "What the devil are you doing here? I have been looking for you everywhere!"

"Williams and I are making sure the cellars are adequately stocked," Portia replied, handing the bottle to the silent butler. "Is there something amiss?" She wondered if he had come to ask about his mother, and prayed he had not. So far the countess had yet to begin her "recovery," and Portia was wondering if the older woman was going to call her bluff.

"Never mind that now," he said, ignoring her question and reaching out to capture her hand. "I want you to come with me."

Before she could say another word he was leading her up the steps, his warm hand holding hers in a firm grip.

"Where are we going?" she demanded, holding up her skirts as she struggled to keep up with his longer strides.

"To the ballroom," he replied, not bothering to turn around. "There is something I want to show you."

The chandelier, she thought miserably, recalling she hadn't had time to have the thing cleaned. She was trying to think of some plausible excuse to offer when they walked into the huge, sunlit room, and the sight of a small, bespectacled lady sitting at the pianoforte brought her up short.

"This is Miss Bixley," he said, nodding at the white-haired lady. "She teaches music at one of local ladies' seminaries, and she has kindly consented to play for us so that we might learn the waltz. Have you not, Miss Bixley?"

His warm smile set the older lady to blushing like a debutante. "Oh, yes, my lord," she gushed in a soft voice. "I shall be only too happy to oblige you."

"Good." He turned to Portia, the gleam in his eyes daring her to object. "Now, although I have never performed the waltz I'm not quite such a savage that I am completely unfamiliar with it. I believe I am to hold my partner . . . so." He slipped his arm about her waist and drew her against him. "Is this correct?"

Portia's cheeks grew as flushed as Miss Bixley's at the feel of his hard, muscled chest brushing against her. "I . . . yes, my lord, only perhaps not so tightly," she suggested, thinking he felt a great deal different from the shy, diffident young man she had bullied into teaching her the scandalous dance.

"Is this better?" He loosened his hold slightly.

She moved back a pace. "Yes, my lord," she replied, heaving a silent sigh of relief.

If he noticed she sounded a trifle breathless, he was too much of a gentleman to comment. Instead he took her right hand in his, his fingers curling about hers intimately. "And if I recall correctly, I am to hold your hand," he said, his breath stirring the hair on top of her head.

The way her heart was racing was almost as disconcerting as his touch, and Portia stoically ignored both sensations. She had the sneaking suspicion Connor was purposefully attempting to rattle her, and she refused to let him know he was succeeding. Drawing a deep breath to steady her pulse, she turned to the schoolteacher, who was watching the unfolding drama with avid interest. "If you would start playing, Miss Bixley, we shall begin," she said coolly, and then turned back to Connor.

"Listen to the music," she instructed, her gaze fixed on the cravat inches from her nose. "If

you've ever danced the minuet you will recognize
the cadence. Do you hear it?"

He listened intently. "I believe so," he said at
last, smiling down at her. "My tutors told me I
was gifted musically, and I'm sure I shall be able
to whirl you about a dance floor without disgrac-
ing either of us."

Portia ignored the provocation in his deep voice
and concentrated instead on the front of his shirt.
"The important thing to remember is that your
partner will look to you for guidance," she continued stonily, struggling to hear the music over the
wild pounding of her heart. "She will follow your
lead, and it is important that you learn to signal
your intention without speaking."

"And how do I do that?" he asked, his mocking
tone making it evident that he was amused by the
pedantic way she was describing the "wanton"
waltz.

Portia gritted her teeth at the taunting words.
Had it not been for the presence of Miss Bixley,
she would have relieved her anger by kicking his
shins, or by trodding on his toes. Since those particular reprisals were denied her, she decided to
think of something else.

She raised her eyes to his face, her lips curving
in a smile that was far too innocent to be credible.
"You give her waist a slight squeeze, my lord,"
she said sweetly, her fingers digging into his muscular shoulder, "like this."

He didn't so much as flinch, although she knew
it must hurt like the very devil. In fact, the mischief in his eyes grew even more pronounced as
his eyes met hers in silent battle. "Let me be certain that I understand you, ma'am," he drawled.
"When I wish my lady to turn, I do this." His
hand slipped forward to boldly cup her waist.

Portia did her best not to gasp and pull away.

He wasn't hurting her, but he did apply enough pressure to make her aware of his strength. Conceding temporary defeat, she yielded the field to him with a resentful glare.

"Yes, Lord Doncaster, that is correct," she said, determined to make it through the demonstration with as much dignity as possible. "Shall we begin? One, two, three. One, two, three . . ."

To her surprise the earl was an adept pupil, and after only a few missteps he was soon whirling her about the room with all the grace of a French dancing master. By the time they had completed their third rotation about the dance floor, she was breathless with laughter, her ill humor completely forgotten.

"Fie on you, sir!" she charged teasingly, her eyes sparkling as she tilted back her head to smile at him. "I thought you said you did not waltz!"

"I didn't think I did," he replied, his lips curving in an answering smile. Their gazes met, and in that moment all of time seemed to come to a halt. She could feel the caress of his breath on her cheeks, and the strong beat of the heart that was pressed against her own.

Portia saw his eyes darken to purest emerald, and the passion in their jewel-like depths made her burn with answering fire. Her fingers tightened on his shoulder, her eyes fluttering closed as he began to lower his head toward her.

"Ah, there you are!" A voice from the door shattered the fragile spell, and they broke apart as Lady Eliza, sitting in a new wheelchair, wheeled herself into the room. Connor was the first to recover, and he gave Portia one last burning look before turning toward the door.

"Mother, what are you doing in that thing?" he demanded, hurrying to her side. "Where is your Bath chair?"

"In the attic, where it belongs," the countess retorted, her jaw set in a mutinous line. "Those things are for old ladies in their dotage. Do you think I wish our guests to think me a step away from the grave?"

"Certainly not," he denied, "but—"

"Good." Lady Eliza turned to Portia with a set smile. "There you are, my dear," she said coolly. "Lady Alterwaithe will be here shortly, and you did ask me to remind you so that you could change your gown."

Portia had asked no such thing, but she was too grateful for the distraction to quibble. "Thank you, my lady, I will go and change at once," she said, forcing herself to turn to the earl. "Will you be joining us, sir?"

Connor's gaze remained hooded as he studied her averted face. "I wouldn't dream of missing it," he assured her, his voice rough with an effort to control his emotions.

She gave a jerky nod. "Then if you will excuse me, I shall go to my rooms," she said, and then turned and fled as if all the hounds in hell were pursuing her.

10

L ord and Lady Langwicke and their daughter,
Lady Margaret, were among the first guests
to arrive. The marchioness was an old friend of
the countess's, and they greeted each other like
long-lost sisters. The two ladies retreated to the far
corner of the drawing room to renew their acquaintance, and since Connor had been called
away by an emergency, it fell to Portia to entertain
the marquess and his beautiful daughter. Lord
Langwicke accepted the earl's absence with a mutter and a shrug, but his daughter was more vocal
in her displeasure.

"I must say I am disappointed." Lady Margaret
sighed, her cupid's-bow mouth set in a pretty pout
as she accepted the glass of lemonade Portia offered her. "I have heard so much of his lordship,
and I was quite looking forward to meeting him."

"Lord Doncaster should be home shortly, my
lady," Portia replied politely, wondering what it
was about the lively brunette that set her back up.
"One of the tenants was trampled by a horse, and
he has gone to check on him."

"All of my friends are quite beside themselves
with envy," Lady Margaret prattled on, ignoring
Portia's explanation. "He has not been in town *forever*, and one hears the most delicious stories." She
leaned forward, brown eyes sparkling with mali-

cious curiosity. "Tell me, Miss Haverall, is the earl really as savage as they say he is?"

Portia's hands clenched about her own glass, and she wondered how its contents would look streaming down Lady Margaret's lovely gown. "Lord Doncaster is not in the least a savage," she replied stiffly, setting the lemonade down before she acted on her impulses. "He is no town fop, I grant you, but he is hardly a barbarian. In fact—" She fixed Lady Margaret with a challenging look "—he is an excellent dancer. I have never waltzed with another man half so graceful."

Lady Margaret blinked as if in surprise. "But how can this be?" she asked in the tones of a child just learning there was no Father Christmas. "One hears—"

"One may hear a great many foolish things," Portia interrupted, deciding she'd had about enough of the girl's nonsense, "but it does not necessarily follow that one must believe them. His lordship is your host, and I am sure you are too much of a lady to engage in idle gossip about him."

Lady Margaret's cheeks turned almost as pink as her ruffled muslin gown, and she set her glass down with a bang. "If you will have one of the servants show me to my rooms, I believe I shall retire," she said, rising to her feet with all the dignity an eighteen-year-old could muster. "I have the headache!"

Portia dutifully rang for a maid, but Lady Margaret had no sooner flounced out of the room than a second barouche rolled up in front of the house, and Portia found herself repeating the conversation with another group of giggling, wide-eyed debutantes. By the time these annoying creatures had been put firmly in their place and escorted to their rooms, Portia's temper was beginning to show signs of strain.

"Upon my word, Lady Doncaster," she said, turning to the countess the moment they were alone, "whatever did you write these ladies? They seem to look upon your son as if he was an exhibit in the royal menagerie!"

Lady Eliza's lips twitched at Portia's descriptive imagery. "Well, the dolt has only himself to blame," she said, leaning back in her new wheel-chair with a self-satisfied smile. "He is the one who chose to turn up his nose at society, and we really cannot blame them if they have formed their own opinions of him. Besides, ladies like a bit of mystery in a man. Makes 'em seem more dashing than they really are."

"A bit of mystery is one thing. Being regarded as one step removed from a cage is another," Portia retorted, scowling as she recalled one young lady, Miss Anne Derwynn, shivering in ecstatic horror at the thought of meeting the Black Earl.

"Nonsense, child, you refine too much on society's tattle," Lady Eliza assured her with a patronizing smile. "Now, if these chits were yawning at the mention of Connor's name, *then* we would have cause for alarm. As it is . . ." She shrugged her shoulders expressively.

Portia said no more, although she vowed to have a discreet word with Connor so that he would know what to expect. If the younger ladies began swooning and acting as if they expected to be ravished on the spot, she would never get him to venture out again. He would doubtlessly retreat into one of his dark silences, and the entire house party would end in disaster.

The traitorous thought came to her that this might be all to her advantage, but she ruthlessly refused to acknowledge it. The objective of this little gathering was to help Connor establish himself in society, and she was determined to do just that. The only difficulty would be in convincing him not to fly into the boughs the first time one of the chits called him "The Black Earl" to his face. But how? The problem kept her mind occupied as she braced herself to receive the next wave of visitors.

Connor's shoulders were slumping with weariness as he walked down the back hallway from the kitchens. It had been a hellish day, and he longed for the privacy of his room and an hour or two of blessed silence. Unfortunately, with a house filled with guests, this was a luxury he would have to do without, and even as he was cursing this fact the door to one of the parlors opened, and a woman stepped out, almost colliding with him. He opened his mouth to utter an automatic apology when he recognized Portia.

"Have a care, madam," he warned, reaching out to steady her. "This isn't a racetrack, you know."

"Connor!" she exclaimed, and the sound of his name on her lips pleased him more than he dared admit.

"And a good thing for you, too," he said, making no move to stand aside so that she could pass. "If I had been one of our guests, you may have sent me tumbling. For once, 'twould seem my size has its advantages."

She smiled slightly, but instead of responding with an answering quip as he expected, she laid her hand on his arm. "Is everything all right?" she asked in a quiet voice, her misty gray eyes searching his face. "How is the man who was injured?"

Rather than prevaricating or sheltering her from the grim reality, Connor answered truthfully, knowing she would understand. "Alive, thank God, although it will be months yet before he can walk," he replied, some of his weariness vanishing at her comforting touch. He'd spent the morning helping hold down the man while his shattered leg was set, and he could still hear the man's agonized groans. He pushed the grisly scene from his mind and gazed down at Portia, noting her appearance with pleasure.

She had stopped wearing her mourning clothes some weeks ago, but this was the first time he'd seen her so fashionably dressed, and he thought her yellow gown of striped muslin enchanting. "How is everything here? Have the guests arrived?" he asked, noting a dark curl had come undone from her chignon, and wishing he could tuck it back into place.

The mention of the guests seemed to recall Portia to the proprieties, and she dropped her hand from his arm, taking a hasty step back from him. "I am glad you mentioned the guests," she said, her eyes fixed on the front of his jacket. "I feel I really ought to warn you."

"Warn me?" he repeated, frowning in confusion. "What on earth are you talking about?"

She remained silent for so long, he wondered if she meant to ignore him. He was about to press for an explanation when she gave an uneasy laugh. "It would seem that the clergy was right, my lord, and that reading Byron does have a most lamentable effect on female minds," she said, her falsely light tone making his eyes narrow in suspicion.

"Meaning?" he asked, certain he would not care for whatever she was about to say.

"Meaning that you, sir, have been cast in our younger guests' minds as the very epitome of some of the baron's more interesting heroic characters."

"What?"

"Come, now." She gave another laugh, still managing to avoid his gaze. "You must know the ladies regard you as a dark and mysterious lord. To them you are the stuff of legends, and they are completely in awe of you. I . . . I merely thought you would wish to know."

Connor felt his cheeks heat with embarrassment. He'd dreaded being stared at as if he was some sort of freak, but the last thing he expected was that he should be regarded as some sort of dashing, romantic figure. The thought was so startling that a reluctant smile began to spread across his face.

"Byron?" he asked, his lips twitching as he gazed down at her.

"Undoubtedly. His lordship's epic poems are the rage amongst the young ladies," she said, finally raising her eyes to his. "If you want my opinion, they are already half in love with you. Your mother tells me there is nothing like a dark and mysterious reputation to make a lady go weak in the knees. We shall doubtlessly have to send to York for an entire vat of smelling salts if we mean to make it through the next fortnight."

He laughed at the image, his spirits lifting. Suddenly the thought of Hawkshurst being overrun with visitors was not so daunting, Connor realized as he escorted Portia down the hall.

In honor of the guests' first night at Hawkshurst, several members of the local gentry had been invited to dinner. Portia was relieved to see that Miss DeCamp had accepted her invitation. She was looking as lovely as ever in a modest gown of topaz satin, her dark-blonde hair gathered back in a love knot. When Portia complimented her on her toilet, the other girl flashed her a grateful smile.

"It is very kind of you to say so, Miss Haverall," she said, her brown eyes flicking wistfully toward Lady Margaret, who was dressed in a stunning gown of white silk festooned with pink rosebuds. "But I fear I may be a trifle underdressed."

Portia also gazed at the pretty brunette, thinking she looked more like a piece of confectionery than a real person. She was also flirting shamelessly with the earl, who, she noted sourly, was bearing up under the assault quite nicely.

"Her ladyship is young yet, and so we must forgive her her excesses," she said, keeping her voice pitched low so that the catty remark would not be overheard. "I am only surprised her mama allowed her to wear something so inappropriate."

Miss DeCamp's gaze flicked to the marchioness, who was occupying the seat of honor to Connor's left. "I'm not," she said, and then covered her mouth with her hand, sending Portia a horrified look.

"I cannot believe I said that," she whispered, her cheeks going pink with embarrassment. "I have never said anything so mean-spirited in all my life!"

"Posh!" Portia replied gruffly, feeling rather like a black-hearted sinner who had just corrupted an innocent. "If you could have heard the way her ladyship and her beauteous daughter were dishing up the cream with the other cats, you would not feel so guilty. Besides," she added, eyeing the jewel-bedecked marchioness with distaste, "it is nothing less than the truth."

"What are the two of you whispering about?" Lady Eliza demanded, her expression full of curiosity. "You have been sitting there with your heads together forever!"

"We were talking about York, my lady," Portia answered, uttering the falsehood without so much as turning a hair. "Miss DeCamp was just telling me it also has several Roman ruins that might be of interest to our guests."

"You must be referring to the base of the minster and the old tower," the Honorable Keegan McLean replied calmly, giving both ladies an encouraging smile. "They are said to have been part of the *principia*."

"What is that?" Portia asked, grateful for his assistance. She had met him earlier that evening, and found him most charming. Despite his elegant looks he was surprisingly friendly, and she could see why the earl was so fond of him.

"The garrison headquarters. York was once the military capital of Britain," he supplied, his hazel eyes resting on Miss DeCamp. "I had no idea you were interested in the Romans, Miss DeCamp."

"There is much about me, sir, which you do not know," Miss DeCamp returned. "But yes, it is an interest of mine. As I believe it is an interest of yours, my lord?" she added, turning her shoulder on Mr. McLean as she gazed at Connor.

"As a matter of fact, it is," Connor replied with a smile.

"Perhaps we might all ride into town tomorrow and view these ruins," Lady Langwicke suggested, her expression stern as she frowned at her daughter, obviously annoyed she was allowing another young lady to be the center of so much masculine attention. "My daughter is equally fond of ruins, aren't you, dearest?"

Lady Margaret was quick to pick up on her mama's prodding. "Oh, yes," she gushed, flashing Connor a melting smile. "I quite adore them!"

"Are they haunted?" Miss Derwynn demanded from her place halfway down the table. "I am sure they must be! One of my favorite novels was set in

a ruined chapel, and it had the most evil spirit in
it. I vow, I could scarcely bear to finish it!"

Her mention of novels reminded Portia of her
conversation with Connor, and she risked meeting
his eyes. As she expected, they were dancing with
silent laughter, and for a moment they shared the
private joke. When he turned his attention to Miss
Derwynn, however, his mien was as somber as always.

"As to the presence of spirits, ma'am, I cannot
say, but the minster is spectacular. If everyone is
agreeable, I am sure we can arrange something."

The topic of the proposed trip occupied the conversation for the rest of the meal, and by the time
the ladies rose to leave the gentlemen to their port,
everyone was in a surprisingly cordial mood. The
ladies retired to the drawing room, enjoying a
cozy gossip until the gentlemen rejoined them. Because so many of the guests had traveled a great
distance, it was decided there would be no card
playing that night, and the party soon broke up.
Miss DeCamp and her cousin, who acted as her
chaperone, also decided to return home, and a
small battle of wills ensued when Mr. McLean insisted upon acting as her escort.

"You are very kind, sir," Miss DeCamp said, her
frosty voice belying her polite words, "but it is unnecessary, I assure you. Mrs. Thorn and I managed
to drive here without being attacked, and one may
only assume we shall be able to make the return
trip also unmolested."

"Then perhaps it is I who should seek protection
from you," Mr. McLean returned, his eyes filled
with lazy provocation as he grinned at her. "Besides, as we are both returning along the same
road, it only makes sense that we travel together.
Unless you object to my company?" He raised a
mocking eyebrow at her.

Faced with so direct a challenge there was nothing Miss DeCamp could do but acquiesce, and after bidding her hosts and Portia a stiff good night, she left the room in a flurry of satin skirts. Portia stared at her, wondering what ailed the usually well-behaved young woman. Unfortunately, the squire and the Darlingtons were also busy taking their leave, and she was unable to satisfy her curiosity. Finally they were alone, and the countess collapsed against her chair with a sigh.

"Thank heavens that is over," she said, fanning herself and looking harried. "I cannot think what I was about to invite so many people here, and this is only *half* of them!"

"Are you all right, ma'am?" Connor asked, studying his mother with worry.

Lady Eliza took instant umbrage to his words. "Of course I am!" she snapped, drawing herself upright in her chair. "I am not so aged that a dinner party is enough to put me in my grave! Now, are you going into York tomorrow, or was that all talk to appease the ladies?"

Connor looked as if he were trying not to laugh at the sharp words. "I *was* planning a trip to York, although not necessarily tomorrow," he answered.

"Why not tomorrow?" the countess demanded. "Wasn't it that impertinent Franklin fellow who said that we should never leave until tomorrow that which we should do today? If it is good enough for an American, it ought to be good enough for you."

He accepted his defeat with a good-natured bow. "As you say, my lady. I will see what I can do."

"Good." The countess next turned her sharp gaze on Portia. "Will you be going with them?"

"I'd thought to, yes," Portia replied, enjoying

the sight of Connor being bear-led by his mama. "But if I am needed here—"

"Of course you are needed," the countess interrupted, "which is precisely why you must go. You've been working like a Trojan this past week, and a bit of exercise is just what you need to put some color back in your cheeks. Besides," she added as if in afterthought, "you can help act as duenna for the younger ladies."

Connor's indulgent smile became a frown. "Miss Haverall is our guest, Mother," he said in a reproving tone. "It hardly seems proper we should expect her to sing for her supper. I am sure Lady Langwicke and the other mamas will provide adequate protection."

Lady Eliza lifted her gaze heavenward as if in exasperation. "As you wish," she said in a weary voice. "I am sure you know what is best."

They spent the next quarter hour chatting idly, and the countess kept them entertained as she ruthlessly dissected each guest's foibles. Even Connor joined in, and his wry observations had Portia chuckling in delight. They continued talking even after the countess had taken her leave, and time slid silently away without either of them being aware of it. Portia was only gradually becoming aware of its passage when Connor startled her by suddenly leaning forward to capture her hand in his.

"I wish you would do me the honor of addressing me by my Christian name," he said, his tone serious as he met her gaze. "We have long since passed the need for such stuffy formalities."

Portia's heart leaped at his words and the feel of his hand cradling hers. "I . . . I would like that . . . Connor," she stammered, savoring the sound of his name on her lips. "And I also give you leave to make use of my given name, if you wish."

"I wish," he said, giving her hand a parting squeeze before leaning back in his chair. "And now that we are on such intimate terms, perhaps you will tell me what you and Miss DeCamp were really discussing at the dinner table. And don't attempt to feed me that fustian about York," he added at her incredulous look. "I saw your face, my dear, and I know you weren't discussing anything as prosaic as Roman ruins."

Portia did not know what disconcerted her more, his casual use of the endearment or his acuity in gauging her expression. Evidently he was even more sharp-eyed than she knew, she decided, shooting him a resentful look from beneath her lashes.

"Actually, my lord," she began, making deliberate use of his title to indicate her displeasure, "we were discussing something even more prosaic than antiquities."

"And what might that have been?" he drawled, his eyes gleaming with amusement.

"Fashion," Portia said, supplying the half-truth with a satisfied smile. "Miss DeCamp was afraid her toilet was inadequate for the occasion, and I was but reassuring her. Does that satisfy your curiosity, sir?"

"For the moment," he said, wondering what she would do if he were to kiss that defiant pout from her sweet mouth. The thought was one that had occupied his mind for more days than he could count, and suddenly he knew he could not live another day without learning the truth for himself. Setting aside the scruples he had spent a lifetime acquiring, he leaned forward, taking her hand and drawing her against him as he rose slowly to his feet.

"Connor!" Portia gasped, her hands fluttering to

his massive shoulders. "What on earth do you think you are doing?"

"Do you mean you do not know?" Her breathless question amused him. "Come, Portia, you cannot be *that* green."

Portia glanced up at him, a storm of emotion raging inside her as his arms slowly slid about her. She wasn't afraid, she told herself, and certainly desire could not account for the weakness threatening her to turn her knees to water. Fearing he was making a game of her, she pushed against his broad chest in an effort to secure her freedom.

"If you are trying to intimidate me into confessing, then you may think again!" she said, hiding her confusion behind a dark scowl. "I am not a school-miss to swoon at the sight of you!"

"I am glad to hear that." He laughed, ignoring her struggles and bending his head to catch the softness of her perfume. He could sense she was confused rather than genuinely afraid, and he breathed a silent sigh of relief. The last thing he wanted was to frighten her.

Portia heard the amusement in his voice, and it made her burn with humiliation. She wanted to believe his desire for her was as real as hers was for him, and the realization made her weak with longing. To want him this badly and have him reject her would be as devastating as her father's final rejection, and she did not know if she could bear it.

"I mean it, Connor," she said, her voice trembling as she met his lambent gaze. "If you are trying to bully me . . ."

He gave a soft chuckle, his arms tightening about her slender waist and lifting her against him. "I am not trying to bully you," he denied, his lips hovering inches from hers. "I am trying to kiss you." And with that he bent his head, closing the distance from his mouth to hers.

The first taste of her lips was all that he thought it would be. Sweet, so unbearably sweet, and ripe with the promise of the rapture yet to come. His body clenched with passion, and he longed to pull her even closer and allow his desires full rein. He had never wanted a woman more, and the thought of letting her go was enough to make him groan with frustration. Only the thought of his honor and her reputation kept him from deepening the kiss, and he was shaking with the need for control as he slowly drew back.

"I have been wanting to do that since I first awakened to find you standing over me with that bed warmer in your hand," he murmured in a rueful voice, brushing back a stray curl from her forehead. "You are a dangerous temptation, my sweet."

His soft words of praise made Portia's cheeks warm with delight. She supposed she should slap his face for such presumption, but she was too bemused to make the attempt. And too honest, she admitted, her color deepening as she remembered her response. She glanced away from him uncertainly, suddenly unable to hold his gaze.

"Connor, I—"

"No," he interrupted, resting his thumb on the underside of her jaw as he tipped her face up to his. "I know this should not have happened," he said, his thumb moving in a small circle against the heated flesh, "but I am not going to pretend that I regret it. I only hope you feel the same way. Do you?" He surveyed her anxiously.

Touched by his concern, she reached up and covered his hand with her own, pressing it to her cheek. "I regret nothing," she said softly, meeting his gaze with quiet conviction.

He let out the breath he had been holding. "Good," she said, his thumb moving over her soft lips. "I couldn't bear it if you regretted anything that happened between us." He replaced his thumb with his mouth, indulging in a quick kiss before stepping back again.

"Perhaps it would be best if we said good night," he said, his eyes burning in his face as he gave her one last look. "So will you be accompanying us tomorrow?"

It took a moment for his words to penetrate the sensual fog filling Portia's mind. "I . . . I was going to, yes," she said, praying he wouldn't ask her to stay home. She had to see him again, even if they were surrounded by a dozen people.

He gave a curt nod, his hands clenched at his sides. "I shall see you then," he said, his voice still rough with passion. "Good night, Portia."

Portia spent a restless night reliving the kiss, and dreaming of Connor. She remembered the taste of his warm mouth on hers, and the feel of his hard, muscular body pressed so intimately against her own, and she trembled with thwarted passion. Thank heavens he had been gentleman enough to end the embrace when he had, she mused, turning onto her back with a sigh. She shuddered to think of what might have happened had he not been so noble.

It wasn't as if she'd never been kissed before, she fretted, frowning at the ceiling. She wasn't a wanton by any means, but neither was she a complete innocent. There had been a few stolen kisses here and there throughout her girlhood, but this was the first time a simple kiss had ever made her forget everything but the man holding her. Connor had made her feel things she had never felt before, and she greatly feared she had been on the verge

of surrendering more than her honor to him. She
feared she had been about to offer him her heart
as well.

She awoke late the next morning, bleary-eyed
and edgy from lack of sleep. Since they weren't
leaving for York until after luncheon, she was able
to avoid the other guests by staying in her study
and pretending to go over the plans for the costume ball. She heard from Nancy that Connor had
gone about his morning chores as usual, but that
he was expected to return by noon. The information made her breathe a silent sigh of relief, and
she prayed she would have her errant emotions in
hand before she must face him again.

They set out for York after luncheon, traveling
in three separate coaches. In honor of the occasion
Portia wore one of her new gowns of cherry-red
muslin, a chip straw bonnet with a matching rib-
bon perched on her curls. A striped parasol and a
pair of crocheted mitts completed the ensemble,
and she felt confident she could hold her own
amongst the well-dressed beauties. That she
should care about such paltry concerns shamed
her, but she took comfort in the fact that she was
finally behaving like a true lady. Her father, she re-
flected with a grim smile, would doubtlessly be
gratified.

In York they went first to the spectacular cathedral where they had arranged to meet Miss De-
Camp and Mr. McLean. Despite her own troubling
thoughts, Portia noted that Miss DeCamp seemed
somewhat distressed, and while the others were
admiring the stained-glass window, she drew her
off for a private coze.

"Is everything all right, Miss DeCamp?" she
asked, studying the other woman with concern.
"You seem a trifle quiet today."

Miss DeCamp flushed guiltily. "I am sorry to be

such poor company," she said, her gaze sliding toward Mr. McLean, "but that wretch has been plaguing me all morning, and I vow, I have reached the end of my endurance!"

The vehemence in her voice startled Portia. "Indeed?" she asked, her own gaze shifting in the man's direction. "Has he been making untoward advances? If so, I am sure Lord Doncaster would be more than happy to have a word with him."

Miss DeCamp gave a nervous start. "It's nothing like that," she said, her color deepening. "It's simply that Mr. McLean is laboring under the misconception that I find his attentions flattering, and he has been making something of a pest of himself. But it is nothing I cannot handle on my own," she added, her chin lifting.

"Well, if you are certain," Portia said, smiling as she recalled her first impression of the other lady. "But if he gives you any further trouble, do not hesitate to inform his lordship. He will soon set the wretch straight."

"If the wretch gives me further trouble I shall push him off Clifford's Tower!" Miss DeCamp muttered with such feeling that Portia feared for the handsome rascal's safety.

While Portia talked to Miss DeCamp, Connor stood listening to Lady Langwicke rhapsodizing over the Rose Window, his hooded gaze never leaving Portia's face. He had always thought her lovely, but looking at her now, standing in the stone nave while a rainbow of colors from the soaring windows washed over her, he thought her the most beautiful woman he had ever seen. As if sensing his perusal she suddenly glanced up, her silver-gray eyes meeting his. For a brief moment time and place faded away, and he gazed at her with all the hunger he could no longer deny.

The memory of their brief kiss had stayed with

him all night and through the long morning. Even as he went about his daily chores he could still taste the honey of her lips, and it had taken all of his considerable control to push the image from his mind. He thought he had succeeded, but gazing at her soft lips now, it was all he could do to keep from closing the distance between them and helping himself to another sweet taste.

Even as the tempting thought was forming in his mind, Portia's cheeks grew pink, and she dropped her gaze and turned away. He was wondering if he should go to her when another group of people came into the cloister, tour books in hand. He started moving to one side when one of the ladies gave a startled gasp.

"My heavens, Lord Doncaster, is that you?" she exclaimed, her indigo eyes wide as she gazed up at him. "Do you not recognize me?" she asked, her lips curving in a reproving smile. "It is me, Olivia! What are you doing here?"

11

At first Connor could not believe the evidence of his own senses. In the years since Olivia's cruel rejection he'd often dreamed of meeting her again. He had wiled away many a lonely night imagining what he would say, and how he would behave should they ever meet. But now that the moment had actually arrived, he was too numb to do anything other than stare at her. Aware he was becoming the object of everyone's attention, he quickly shook off his shock.

"Good afternoon, Lady Duxford," he said coolly, managing a polite bow. "I had no idea you and your husband were in town. I trust you are well?"

The eyes he had once thought bluer than the most costly of sapphires sparkled with amusement. "Oh, dear," she said, her pink lips curving in a moue, "I am really not certain how I should answer. *I* am quite well, but I fear my poor husband is not. He died well over a year ago."

Connor's cheeks reddened in embarrassment, and he felt as gauche and awkward as he had felt at twenty. "My apologies, my lady, I had not heard," he said, his new cravat suddenly seeming much too tight. "Pray accept my condolences for your sad loss."

"You are too kind," the marchioness responded, unfolding her fan in a languid gesture. "But as I say, it has been over a year, and I have had time to accept that I am all alone in the world. But what of you? Whatever brings you to York, and in the company of so many lovely ladies? I heard you had become something of a recluse, and never left your estate."

"His lordship is kindly showing us about the town," Portia answered for him, deciding she'd had enough of the pretty blonde and her simpering ways. She remembered the countess saying Lady Duxford was a beauty, but that in no way prepared for the stunning lady in her perfectly matched silks and velvets.

Lady Duxford's eyes narrowed on Portia. "Is he indeed?"' she purred, her soft voice reminding Portia of a coiled snake about to strike. "In that case, perhaps you will allow my friends and me to join you? So far it has been a dreadfully dull day."

It was obvious this observation did not sit well with the three young dandies escorting the marchioness. Nor did the mamas in the group seem eager to welcome the widow and her entourage in their little group. However, there was no graceful way they could refuse, and when Lady Duxford twined her arm through the earl's, there seemed nothing left to do.

"Forward creature," Portia heard Lady Langwicke whisper to one of the other mamas. "It would seem those rumors one hears are the truth. Indeed," she added, bristling as the marchioness threw back her head and gave a merry laugh, "it would seem they do not even begin to do her justice."

"One dislikes speaking ill of the dead," Mrs. Darlington said, the smug note in her voice belying the prim words, "but I heard her husband actually *encouraged* her outrageous behavior. My husband says he even vetted her lovers, and that he . . ." She lowered her voice, apparently wishing to spare any innocent ears from the juicy details she was imparting with such relish.

Portia could have shrieked with frustration. She had never been one to engage in idle gossip, but something about the marchioness made her want to learn all she could. Perhaps it was the way she seemed discontent to have but one man's attention, and was brazenly flirting with Mr. McLean even as she clung possessively to the earl's arm. The sight made Portia clench her teeth in anger, and she wondered if anyone would object were she to bash the other woman over the head with her reticule.

While Portia was busy plotting, Connor was wrestling with his own troubling thoughts. Now that he'd recovered from his initial shock, he was beginning to sort out his turbulent emotions. He realized that rather than being filled with bitter anger or wild joy, he felt only indifference, and a vague sense of relief. He was no longer blindly infatuated with Olivia's beauty, and without that infatuation he could see her for what she was, and he thanked God she had had the good sense to refuse him. He shuddered to think what his life might have been like married to such a cold and calculating little jade.

"You are rather quiet, my lord," Olivia chastised him, her hand tightening on his arm as they walked slightly ahead of the rest of the group. "May I ask what you are thinking?"

Connor glanced down into her face, wondering coolly how long that inviting smile would last if he answered her honestly. For a brief moment he was strongly tempted to do just that, but in the end he called upon the hard control that had stood him in such good stead over the years.

"I was thinking, my lady, that I ought to make

more of an effort to get into town," he prevaricated, his gaze moving away from hers. "This is the first visit I have made to the minster since my father's death some five years ago."

"Oh." It was obvious his cool reply was not what she expected, and there was a long pause before she made another try. "I hear there is to be an assembly tomorrow night," she said in a bored tone. "Of course, country entertainments can be *so* tiresome, but if you are going, perhaps I will as well." She shot him a languid look ripe with enticement. "Perhaps we might even keep each other entertained, my lord?" she added, her dimples flashing.

Connor remembered how the sight of those dimples had once made him weak-kneed. "As I will be acting as host to our guests, I fear I shall have little time to call my own," he said, amused at how the tables had been turned. Where once he would have done anything to win a smile from her, she now seemed equally anxious to fix his interest with her. It might be interesting to play along, and see how far she meant to go, he thought, and reached a swift conclusion.

"But that is not to say that every moment of my evening will be taken up with duty dances," he added, raising her hand to his lips for a brief kiss. "I am sure I shall find some time for . . . such an old friend."

For a moment he feared he had overplayed his hand, but then her enchanting smile dawned, and she gave a throaty laugh. "I would rather you refer to me as your *dear* friend," she corrected, bringing her long lashes into play as she gazed up at him. "*Old* friend has such an unfortunate connotation, do you not agree?"

"As if one could ever take you for anything other than a fresh-faced debutante," he riposted, delighting her and surprising himself. He'd never been so glib in his youth, and he was amazed at how easy it was. He remembered all the light and teasing conversations he'd had with Portia, and realized that she was responsible for his newfound confidence.

Without his being aware of it she'd made him lower the shield he'd always held between himself and the rest of the world. But rather than feeling vulnerable at the sudden lack of protection, he felt oddly free. The realization made him forget all about the woman on his arm, and he longed to return to Hawkshurst to share it with Portia. Unfortunately he first had to think of some way to extract himself from Olivia's coils.

He was mulling over various possibilities when one of the dandies, Sir Cecil Chessfield, stiffly reminded Olivia they were expected elsewhere for tea. The look Olivia shot the hapless man made it plain he had displeased her, but she was all sweetness and charm when she turned back to Connor.

"Duty calls," she said, holding her hand out to him. "I shall look forward to seeing you tomorrow night."

Connor's eyes sparkled as he bent over the offered hand. "As shall I, Lady Duxford," he said suavely. "As shall I."

They returned to Hawkshurst in far lower spirits than they had set out, and Portia was not surprised when half the guests laid claim to the headache and retired to their rooms. Heaven knew she would like to indulge in a similar malady, but as Lady Duxford had said, duty called. Portia paused only long enough to wash her face and hands, and then hurried down to the parlor where Lady Eliza was impatiently waiting for a report.

"Well, what happened?" the countess demanded

the moment Portia entered the room. "Did Connor single out any particular lady for his attentions?"

"You might say that," Portia replied with a sigh as she took her chair across from her. "He showed a marked performance for one lady, and I saw him kiss her hand at least twice."

"Really?" Lady Eliza beamed with delight. "Was it that nice Miss DeCamp? I did say the two of them were well-suited, did I not?"

"So you did. Unfortunately, Miss DeCamp was not the object of his lordship's attentions."

"Never say he was making up to one of those tiresome Darlington chits," Lady Eliza demanded with a scowl. "They are sweet enough, but years too young for him. I would not have it bandied about that Connor snatched his bride from the cradle."

An ironic smile lit Portia's eyes. "Indeed not," she assured the countess in a quiet tone. "The lady in question is of a more mature nature; closer to his lordship's age in fact."

"Really?" The countess looked puzzled. "I cannot recall any of the ladies being so old as that, unless he was dangling after one of the mamas?" She glanced at Portia in apprehension.

"No, my lady," Portia said, the image of Connor chasing Lady Langwicke about the cloisters almost enough to lift her spirits.

"Then blast it all, who was she?" Lady Eliza snapped, losing all patience.

"Lady Olivia Duxford."

Lady Eliza gaped at her in horror. "What?" she cried, her hands fluttering to her throat. "No, it cannot be. If you are twigging me, Portia, I vow I shall be quite cross with you!"

Portia gave a dispirited sigh. "I'm not teasing, my lady," she said, her shoulders slumping in defeat. "I only wish I were." And she proceeded to tell Lady Eliza every detail of the unfortunate encounter.

"And do you mean to say my son encouraged this hussy?" the countess said once Portia had finished. "I refuse to believe it! He cannot be so lacking in pride as all that!"

"I told you we should have informed him of the marchioness's arrival," Portia reminded her unhappily. "If he had known she was in the neighborhood he would have had time to prepare himself. As it was, he simply turned around and there she was."

Lady Eliza scowled at the hint that she was somehow to blame for the contretemps. "I still do not see how it would have mattered one way or another, especially if he is as besotted with the creature as you say he is," she grumbled, clearly furious at the upheaval in her carefully laid plans.

"I did not say he was besotted," Portia corrected, feeling an odd pain in the region of her heart. Only last night Connor had held her in his arms, his mouth burning hers with his ardor, and today he seemed to have forgotten her very existence. Oh, he'd been polite enough, she supposed, but on the ride back from York he had seemed distracted and moody, and it took very little imagination to know what . . . or rather *who* occupied his thoughts. The knowledge made her throat ache with unshed tears.

" . . . going through," the countess concluded with a weary sigh, and Portia realized she had missed something. Rather than admit as much she gave the older lady a puzzled look.

"What do you mean, ma'am?" she asked with credible calm.

"Merely that for all he is a man, my son is no fool," Lady Eliza said calmly. "He may think he loves her as he did when he was a youth, but once he sees her for the scheming minx she is, he will soon realize it is nothing more than the last flicker of lost love."

Portia wished she could believe it was as simple as that. She *knew* Connor, knew he wasn't a callow youth at the mercy of his emotions. He was a man in every sense of the word, and if he gave his heart to a woman, it would be done in full knowledge of what he was doing, and it would be forever. The thought was depressing enough to make her hands tremble and her cup rattle on the saucer.

"My word, Portia, are you all right?" Lady Eliza asked, eyeing her with concern. "You aren't feeling faint, are you?"

"No, my lady, it is nothing like that," she said, setting the cup on the side table with great care. "I have a slight headache, that is all."

"Then you must go to your rooms at once," Lady Eliza said with alacrity. "You should never have come down in the first place."

"But the guests . . ."

"Oh, pooh!" the countess declared with a stern look. "I have been handling guests since you were in leading strings. Not that there will be so many of them, mind," she added with a knowing smirk. "Your headache seems to be catching."

Portia ignored the jibe. "If you are certain it will not be an inconvenience, I *would* like to retire," she said, rising to her feet. "But if you should have need of me, you have only to send for me and I shall come right down."

The countess leaned forward to give her hand a loving pat. "You go on up, child," she said softly. "If worse comes to worst, I shall send for Connor. It is about time he started doing his duty by his guests."

Portia blinked back tears at the older woman's

kindness. "You are very good to me, my lady," she said, bending to brush a kiss across the countess's cheek. "Good afternoon."

Lady Eliza watched Portia leave, her own eyes misting with tears. The moment she was alone she pulled out the miniature of her husband she wore about her neck. "Blast it, Doncaster," she said, addressing her beloved's painted features with a frown, "what are we going to do now?"

"So this is where you have hidden yourself," Connor teased, smiling as he came upon Portia picking flowers the following afternoon. It was the first time he had seen her since their ill-fated visit to York, and until this moment he hadn't realized he'd been looking for her. She was wearing a simple gown of lavender and cream silk, and he thought she looked as lovely as the blooms in her basket.

"Good afternoon, my lord," she said, her tone as cool as the gray eyes that peeked up at him from beneath the wide brim of her straw bonnet. "Was there something that you wanted?"

Her tone as well as her use of his title made him arch his eyebrow in surprise. "To begin with, you may call me Connor, as you have already promised you would," he said, reaching out to pluck from her fingers the rose she had just cut. Holding her gaze with his, he lifted the flower to his nose and inhaled its sweet fragrance. He then kissed the soft petals, and handed it back to her without saying another word.

To his delight the symbolism of his gesture was not lost on her, for she flushed a bright-pink. "As you wish ... Connor," she said, turning away and busying herself with the flowers. "Is there anything else you wished? Lady Langwicke is anxious

that I get these flowers cut by mid-afternoon so
that we can make bouquets for all the ladies."

Connor was uncertain how to respond. Less
than two nights ago they had held each other in a
passionate embrace, and now she was treating him
as if he was nothing but a chance acquaintance.
Her actions made him want to pull her back into
his arms and remind her that he was much more
than that, but logic told him this was neither the
time nor the place. Not that he intended letting the
matter pass unchallenged, he decided, removing
the clippers from her fingers and cutting a single
white rose.

"Will you be attending the assembly with us?"
he asked, the rose dangling from his fingers.

The question made her frown in confusion. "Of
course I am," she replied, tilting her chin up as she
met his gaze. "You made me promise to waltz
with you, remember?"

"I do," he answered, his voice husky, "but I
thought perhaps you might have forgotten . . .
along with a few other things."

"What other things?"

He only smiled at the querulous demand. "I will
tell you later," he promised. "What color is your
ball gown?"

"My ball gown? It is ruby-colored, but I—"

"Then wear this," he instructed, handing her the
dew-dappled blossom.

"Why should I?" Portia asked, accepting the
rose with a suspicious scowl.

"Effect, for one thing," he said, trying not to
smile at her cross expression. "It will make a stunning contrast."

"And the other reason?" she pressed when he
did not elaborate.

"It will tell me that you are thinking about me,"
he answered softly, "as I will be thinking about

you." He caught her hand in his and raised it to his lips for a kiss.

Their gazes met, and in the silvery depths of her eyes he saw a reflection of the same inner turmoil and searing need that were tormenting him. His fingers tightened on hers, and for a briefest moment he wanted to say to the devil with his pride, and pull her into his arms. Only the knowledge that it wasn't just his honor he would be risking prevented him from doing just that, and he reluctantly let her go, feeling more alone and confused than he had ever felt in his life.

After fleeing from the gardens Portia retired to her rooms to brood over Connor's behavior. She was furious with him for flirting with her, and more furious still with herself for being captivated by his polished charm. Until yesterday he was the last man she would have labeled a rake, but now she was not so certain. Surely only a man of low principles would kiss one woman in the moonlight one night, and then make up to his lost love the next morning, she decided, tears shimmering in her eyes as she gazed out the window.

Lost love. The term made her wince. When Connor had kissed her, that was precisely what he thought Lady Duxford was to him. Perhaps if he'd known she was in the area and now free from her marriage to another man, he would never have touched her, Portia. And yet, her logical mind argued silently, such reasoning did not explain his actions this afternoon. He'd been well-aware of Lady Duxford, and he'd still kissed her own hand, his eyes filled with desire.

Did he care for her, she wondered painfully, or was he merely toying with her? She wished she knew, and she wished she knew what the devil she was going to do about it.

She was no closer to resolving these puzzling matters when Nancy came in to help her change for dinner.

"Becoming a regular society miss, aren't you?" the maid scolded as she helped arrange Portia's dark hair in a coil at the back of her head. "Taking to your rooms with a headache every afternoon, and then dragging about looking pale and delicate for the rest of the day. You'll take to carrying smelling salts and swooning next, I don't wonder."

"Don't lecture, Nancy," Portia said wearily, gazing at her reflection with disinterest. She'd been eagerly waiting for the assembly since yesterday, but now she wondered if the countess would let her cry off. She didn't think she could endure watching Connor waltzing with the marchioness.

"If I didn't lecture you, you would only get worse," Nancy said with a sniff, picking up a necklace of gold filigree inlaid with delicate rubies and clipping it about Portia's neck. "A young woman needs a bit of prompting now and then, and 'tis my duty to see you get it."

"A duty you seem to perform with a great relish," Portia muttered beneath her breath.

"Don't be insolent. You know full well what I mean," Nancy reproved, fastening the matching earrings to Portia's ears. When she was finished she stepped back to admire her handiwork. "There," she said, sounding pleased, "you look fine as fivepence, if I say so myself. I heard Lady Langwicke hinted you should wear one of them dreadful turban things, but I'm glad to see you paid her no mind. You've lovely hair, and 'twould be a shame to hide it."

Portia remembered the conversation with the haughty lady that had taken place over tea that afternoon.

"Of course, there is nothing quite so sad as a lady who will not accept the inevitability of the years," Lady Langwicke had said, fixing Portia with a pointed look. "Unmarried ladies of a certain age should accept their fate, and wear the caps and turbans society deems proper for a spinster. It is far more dignified than going about in a debutante's curls. Don't you agree, Miss Haverall?"

Portia had been feeling rather downcast and sorry for herself, but Lady Langwicke's spiteful words had raised her spirits considerably. There was nothing she liked more than deflating such pomposity, and the older woman had provided her with the perfect opportunity to vent some of her temper. She'd picked up her teacup, her lips curved in a sweet smile as she said, "Indeed I do, my lady, and I am glad to see your daughter has the sense to follow your eminently practical advice. That is a lovely cap you are wearing, Lady Margaret," she added, much to that young lady's ire.

"This is not a cap!" she had cried, indicating her lacy head-covering with indignation. "It is a French *chapeau*, and it is all the crack in London!"

"My mistake, then," she had replied in sugary tones, feeling vastly pleased with herself until she'd turned her head and encountered Connor's gaze.

His face had been expressionless, but his eyes had been full of silent laughter. He raised his teacup in a mock salute, and she had felt a closeness to him that was stronger than anything they had ever shared. The memory of that closeness made her catch her breath, and as she gazed into the mirror and saw her reflection, she was at last able to admit the truth. She loved Connor.

* * *

"Good evening, Miss Haverall. That is a beautiful gown you are wearing."

The gentle voice shattered Portia's reverie, and she gazed up from the bench where she had sought sanctuary to find Miss DeCamp standing before her. For a moment she was tempted to ask the young lady, whom she had come to regard as a friend, to go away, but in the end good manners overwhelmed her desire for solitude, and she managed a shaky smile.

"Thank you, Miss DeCamp," she said quietly, sliding over on the bench so that the other girl could join her. "May I say you are also looking quite lovely?"

"If you like," Miss DeCamp replied, settling beside her in a rustle of powder-blue silk. When her skirts were arranged to her satisfaction, she turned to Portia with a warm smile.

"Now that we have been insufferably polite to each other, I wish you would call me Felicity. And your name is Portia, is it not?"

Portia nodded, touched by the other girl's offer of friendship. "Father named me for Brutus's long-suffering wife," she said, forcing herself to think of anything other than the fact that Connor was standing across the ballroom deep in conversation with Lady Duxford.

"Indeed?" Felicity sounded intrigued.

"He was a literature don at Cambridge, and he was teaching *Julius Caesar* to his students when my mother gave birth to me," Portia explained, her eyes twinkling as she remembered the many times she had heard her father tell the story. "I have often given thanks that he was not teaching the comedies at the time, else I might have been saddled with Titania or Thisbee for a name."

"Or Olivia," Felicity said, nodding toward Lady

Duxford. "What do you think Shakespeare would have made of the merry widow in our midst?"

Portia reluctantly followed Felicity's gaze. "Something interesting, I've no doubt," she said, glancing quickly away. "He had a sharp eye."

"And a sharper pen." Felicity unfurled her fan, and began fanning herself in a languid movement. "Mr. McLean told me she was the Duke of Cumbria's mistress, but he threw her over when she began to press for marriage."

The news came as no surprise to Portia, who had taken the widow's measure in one glance. What did surprise her was that Mr. McLean had imparted such shocking news to Felicity. She toyed with her own fan for a few seconds before speaking.

"That doesn't sound like the sort of thing a gentleman should discuss with a lady," she chided, her eyes meeting Felicity's in gentle disapproval.

To her amazement Felicity actually blushed. "You must not blame Mr. McLean," she said, her gaze lowering to her hands. "I fear it was my fault. I had been scolding him for allowing such an obvious creature to wrap him about her pretty finger, and he assured me that I need not have any fear on that score as he had no intention of offering for . . . er . . . shopworn goods." Her color deepened as she repeated the cruel phrase.

Portia wanted to ask her friend why she should be taking her nemesis to task for flirting with another woman, when a shadow fell over them. She glanced up, and her heart stopped when she saw Connor standing before her.

"I have come to claim my waltz," he said in his deep voice, his eyes brilliant as he held out his hand to her. "You did promise it to me, if you recall."

As if she could ever forget, Portia thought, re-

membering the heady sensations she had felt
when he'd first taken her into his arms. Had she
loved him then? she wondered, committing his
handsome features to memory as she gazed up at
him.

"Portia?" His brows gathered in a puzzled
frown. "Do you not wish to waltz?"

The question startled her out of her brown
study, and she rose quickly to her feet. She mumbled a polite apology to Felicity, and allowed
Connor to escort her out onto the dance floor,
where couples were already gathering in eager anticipation.

He slid a firm arm about her waist, his hand
holding hers as they waited for the music to begin.
"I see you are wearing my rose," he said, his voice
pitched to an intimate level as he drew her closer.
"I am glad."

This time Portia was determined not to be
charmed by his sophistry. "As you said, sir, it provided an interesting contrast to my gown," she
said, stiffening slightly and making an attempt to
move back.

He ignored her efforts as if they did not exist,
and held her even closer. "I meant to tell you that
you are looking very beautiful," he said as they
began to move about the room in time to the lilt-
ing music. "I was certain I would have to do battle
with a legion of your suitors in order to claim my
waltz."

Given the fact she'd remained on her bench far
more than she had danced, Portia considered this
a blatant piece of false flattery. She raised her face
to his, fully prepared to unbraid him for uttering
such nonsense. Their eyes clashed, and the expression she saw there had her lowering her own in
confusion. If she hadn't seen him dancing atten-
dance on Lady Duxford a scant few minutes ago,

she would almost think he was captivated by herself, she thought, and then quickly squashed the notion.

She was being ridiculous, she scolded herself. The man was naught but a rake and a flirt, and she would be mad to take his attentions seriously. She thought back to the aloof and difficult man she had first met, and compared him to the handsome and sophisticated man who held her now. Really, she thought sourly, if she had known that her efforts to tame him would have led to this, she would never have bothered!

While Portia was busy silently castigating Connor for his profligate ways, he was busy sorting out his nebulous feelings. He had spent the better part of the evening in Olivia's company, and the more time he had spent with her, the more he wondered how he could ever have thought himself in love with her. Not only was she as spiteful and cruel as he remembered, but she also possessed the morals of a Covent Garden abbess, and it was all he could do not to sneer at the blatant way she kept pressing herself against him. Did she really think him fool enough to take her up on her obvious offer? he wondered bitterly.

It was odd, he mused, but the entire time he had been with Olivia his thoughts had all been on Portia. She looked far more beautiful in her modest gown than Olivia did in her daring dress of gold-shot silk, which was transparent enough to make it obvious she had rouged her nipples. He also could not help but compare their conversation; again, to Portia's credit. While *she* could converse on any number of subjects, Olivia's talk was all of herself, or the latest scandal, and more than once he had found himself fighting a yawn while she had prattled on.

He also could not imagine Olivia bashing him

over the head with a bed warmer, had it been her
room he had burst into when searching for Miss
Montgomery. Indeed, he thought, his lips curving
in a wry smile, it would probably have been he
who would have had to use the bed warmer to
save himself from being ravished. The thought
made him chuckle, and the sound brought a frown
to Portia's face.

"Your lordship finds something amusing?" she
asked, her tone so lofty it was all Connor could do
to keep from kissing her on the spot.

"A great deal, actually," he replied, enjoying the
fire in her eyes. He wondered if he could convince
her to join him for a stroll on the balcony, and was
about to ask when the master of ceremonies came
dashing up to them.

"Lord Doncaster! Lord Doncaster!" the stately
gentleman exclaimed, his normally serene countenance gray with worry. "You must come with me
at once. Your mother has collapsed!"

12

❝I wish everyone would stop fussing, and leave me alone!" Lady Eliza's voice could be heard as Portia and Connor rushed toward the other end of the room where a small crowd had gathered about the woman lying on the floor. Connor roughly shoved one man out of his way, his face white as he knelt beside his mother.

"Are you all right?" he asked gently, taking her hand in his. "What happened?"

"It was the silliest thing, really," she muttered, looking more embarrassed than hurt. "I dropped my reticule, and when I leaned over to pick it up I fell out of my chair. Now kindly help me up. This blasted floor is cold."

The impatient demand relieved Connor of his initial fear that she had reinjured herself, and he bent to pick her up. He was returning her to her chair when she gave a sharp cry.

"My leg!"

He set her down and stepped back. "What is it?" he asked, his eyes filled with concern as he studied her.

"The thing is tingling as if it were afire," Lady Eliza grumbled, her lips twisting into a grimace as she rubbed the affected limb. "I've been feeling occasional twinges, but nothing like this. I must have jolted it when I fell."

Portia had been standing at Connor's side prepared to offer whatever assistance might be required, but at the countess's words she took a step back. So *this* was how she meant to miraculously "recover," she thought, admiration for the other woman's craftiness dispelling the lingering worry for her health. Later she would take the countess to task for her theatrical display, but at the moment she decided it was wisest to get her home before she could dream up even more mischief.

"Perhaps it would be best if we took your mother back to Hawkhurst," she suggested, placing her hand on Connor's arm. "We can arrange to have the doctor meet us there."

Connor hadn't thought about a doctor, but now that she mentioned it, it made sense. He gave a curt nod, and ordered a footman who was hovering nearby to fetch the doctor. After a brief discussion it was decided that those houseguests who wished to do so would remain at the assembly, and less than ten minutes after being summoned to the countess's side, they were on their way back to the estate.

Connor sat across from his mother, taut with anguish, not even aware he was crushing Portia's fingers in his grasp. He kept seeing his mother on the floor, and it reminded him painfully of the accident that had originally injured her. His fault, he thought miserably, all of it was his fault.

"Connor?"

The sound of Portia's voice finally penetrated Connor's misery, and he glanced down to see her watching him. At the same moment he realized he was holding her hand in a tight grip, and he quickly lessened his hold.

"Was I hurting you?" he apologized, rubbing his thumb over her knuckles as if to smooth away the pain. "I'm sorry. There are times when I forget my own strength."

"You weren't hurting me," Portia assured him, although her fingers were throbbing. "I was going to say that you needn't look so grim. Everything will be all right."

When she smiled at him like that, Connor thought, he could believe anything. "I know," he said quietly, carrying the hand he was still clasping to his lips. Their eyes met, and he pressed a grateful kiss to the warm flesh. He would have spoken, but the countess, who had been leaning back on the opposite seat, suddenly stirred to life.

"What are the two of you mumbling about over there?" she demanded crossly. "There's no need to whisper, you know, I'm not that ill!"

Connor and Portia exchanged amused looks as he lowered her hand to her side. "We know you're not, Mother," he said, his deep voice edged with laughter. "We just didn't wish to disturb you with our conversation."

"Conversation, is it?" The countess gave a disbelieving sniff. "Is that what they call it these days?"

They arrived home in less than half an hour, and Connor carried his mother up to her room before leaving her to Portia and the waiting Gwynnen. They undressed Lady Eliza and were doing their best to make her comfortable when the doctor arrived. Connor was resented the way he was shoved gently from the room, but he accepted it with grudging understanding. He went down to the drawing room to wait for news, and was considering ringing for some brandy when the door opened and Portia walked in.

"How is she?" he asked, rushing up to her and grabbing her hand in his. "Is she all right? It's not her heart, is it?"

"No, not at all," Portia assured him, furious with the countess for putting that panicked look in his eyes. She'd taken a moment alone to let her ladyship know what she thought of her charade, but now she wished she'd been more vocal in her disapproval. However pure Lady Eliza claimed her motives to be, she had no right to put her son through such torment.

"Thank God for that," Connor said, his eyes closing as he breathed a sigh of relief. He'd sensed his mother was keeping something from him, and feared she was far more ill than she was letting on. He opened his eyes and smiled at Portia.

"What did the doctor say?" he asked, leading her over to one of the settees and settling easily beside her.

"He is still examining her, but he doesn't seem overly concerned. Indeed, he actually seemed encouraged," Portia replied, feeling even more guilty. Loving Connor and being forced to deceive him was making her miserable, but she didn't see that she had a choice. However distasteful she found such duplicity, she *had* given her word.

"Encouraged?" Connor was frowning at her in concern. "That seems an odd word to use."

Portia stirred slightly, wishing he wasn't so close. "He . . . he thinks the tingling in her legs may be a sign that some feeling is returning to them," she said at last, grateful that in this, at least, she could be completely truthful.

"Do you mean she could walk again?" Connor demanded incredulously.

The happiness in his voice added to Portia's misery. "He did not say, but it seems a logical deduction," she answered quietly, keeping her gaze firmly fastened on the portrait hanging on the far wall.

"But that is wonderful!" Connor exclaimed with

a joyous laugh, gathering her against him for an exuberant hug. When she did not respond, he drew back in consternation. "You don't seem very happy about it," he accused, noting her downcast eyes and pale features.

His quickness made her flinch. "Of course I am happy," she replied, averting her eyes from his too-knowing gaze. "It is just I have been so worried. I suppose the news hasn't sunk in yet." She added this last with an uncomfortable laugh that sounded false even to her own ears.

He gave her a sharp look, and seemed about to press her for more information, but the doctor chose that moment to enter the room. Vowing to get to the bottom of the matter later, he rose to his feet, Portia's hand still held tightly in his.

"How is my mother?" he queried, clinging to Portia's hand as he steeled himself for the doctor's reply.

"Better than I have seen her in years, my lord!" the elderly physician answered, his lined face breaking into a glorious smile. "All feeling has returned to her ladyship's limbs, and it is only a matter of time before she will walk again. A miracle, that is what it is. A miracle!"

The news of Lady Doncaster's recovery spread quickly through the neighborhood, and the house was soon besieged with callers anxious to clap eyes on the miraculously cured invalid. No sooner had one group of curiosity-seekers been ushered out than a second group came dashing in and by mid-afternoon of the second day, Portia's small store of patience had been exhausted. After chasing off a group of church ladies who had come from Easingwold to pray over Lady Eliza, she collapsed on the nearest settee and closed her eyes in weary disgust.

"Well, I hope you are satisfied," she muttered, opening one eye to glare at the countess. "One would think this was the cathedral at Lourdes the way the faithful have been flocking here. A pity we didn't think to charge an admittance fee; we'd all be as rich as Croesus by now."

"Don't be vulgar, my dear," Lady Eliza reproved, fanning herself with languid grace. "I have lived in Yorkshire for the better part of four decades, and it is hardly surprising that my neighbors should express concern over my well-being." She stopped fanning herself and looked thoughtful. "How much do you think we could charge?"

"Never mind," Portia replied, cursing herself for having put the thought in her employer's devious mind. "I still cannot believe you did anything so foolishly melodramatic. Whatever could you have been thinking of? I thought it was agreed you would recover naturally."

"I did," Lady Eliza responded, looking annoyingly smug. "What could be more natural than to be cured by 'the grace and goodwill of God'?"

The quote from one of the church ladies made Portia wince. She had never been particularly religious, but she couldn't help but feel they were risking some form of divine retribution in continuing the deception. "But my lady, I—"

"Oh, do not take on so," Lady Eliza interrupted, snapping her fan closed in annoyance. "I did nothing more than take advantage of my own clumsiness. Or do you think I meant to fall out of that blasted chair?" she added with an angry scowl.

Portia considered this for a long moment. "Do you mean to say it was an accident?" she asked at last.

"Well, of course it was an accident!" the countess exclaimed in frosty accents. "I hope I was raised better than to make a cake of myself in so public a manner!"

Portia was instantly contrite. "I am sorry, your ladyship," she apologized in a soft voice. "I did not mean to insult you."

"Well, I suppose it is of no moment," Lady Eliza continued after an injured pause. "In retrospect it is probably just as well that I acted as I did. Certainly it managed to distract attention from Connor and That Woman."

Portia did not need to be told who That Woman was. The image of Connor flirting with Lady Duxford was burned indelibly in her mind, and it was with a great deal of effort that she forced it from her thoughts.

"It will all be an eight days' wonder, anyway, once the rest of our guests start arriving," Lady Eliza continued in her brisk manner. "And I must say it will be a great relief to be able to participate in the festivities without having to be wheeled about like a sack of grain. Perhaps I might even dance." A smile of anticipation lit her eyes.

They continued chatting for another twenty minutes before their solitude was interrupted by the return of Lady Langwicke and the other guests, who had been off enjoying an impromptu tour of the countryside. Connor accompanied them, and after bending down to kiss her mother's cheek, he shocked Portia by stopping to press a kiss to her hand as well.

"Good afternoon, Miss Haverall," he said, the warm note in his voice making her heart flutter like a schoolgirl's. "Hard at work as usual, I see. We must take care to see you do not become exhausted by taking on too much."

She would not be charmed, Portia told herself sternly. She refused to be charmed by a man who was so fickle in his attentions. "This from a man

who only last week kept us waiting for our dinner
while he was off rescuing a sheep from a hedge-
row," she said, managing a light laugh as she
freed her hand from his. To her relief he let her go,
but that relief was short-lived when he settled on
the chair beside hers.

"Ah, but that was last week. I have since re-
formed," Connor claimed indolently, crossing one
booted foot in front of the other and leaning back
in his chair. He'd spent the entire afternoon waiting to see Portia again, and now he wanted only
to look his fill of her.

She was wearing a gown of ruffled muslin, and
the misty-rose color made her skin glow with life.
Her hair was arranged in a sophisticated knot, but
he remembered how it felt beneath his fingers, and
his hands itched to bury themselves in that silken
softness again. The thought caused his body to respond in an unmistakable manner, and even
though he was somewhat embarrassed by his reaction, he could not help but be wryly relieved.

The other evening Olivia had rubbed herself
against him in a way certain to enflame any man,
and he hadn't felt so much as a stirring of desire.
His lack of response had troubled him, but now he
thought he understood. Evidently his tastes had
become slightly more refined in the last dozen
years, he decided with a rueful grin. He thanked
God for the fact.

The rest of the company seemed oblivious to the
undercurrents swirling about them, and continued
chatting in a desultory manner. Lady Langwicke
had evidently despaired of making a match between Connor and her haughty daughter, and had
now set her sights on one of the young men who
had been invited to round out their numbers.

"The nephew of the Earl of Mayfield, you
know," she confided to Portia in a smug aside.

"Rumor has it that he will name the lad his heir once it is determined his own son is dead."

The explanation shocked Portia enough to make her forget her own troubling emotions. "What do you mean, once it is determined he is dead?" she asked, wondering if she had missed something. "I should think there would be little to debate. A person is either dead, or he is not. How could there be any doubt?"

"Because the son—Adrian was his name—was reported lost at sea when his ship was sunk off the Indies," Lady Langwicke explained with a marked degree of condescension. "Which only goes to show you why an only son ought not to be allowed to gallivant about the globe. It was most thoughtless of the boy to put his own selfish needs above his duty to his title and his family. Do you not agree, my lord?" She turned to the earl with a fatuous smile.

Connor remembered the intense young man who had been the Viscount Comeraugh. Adrian had been two years behind him at Oxford, but he had impressed Connor with both his intelligence and his determination to restore his family fortune. He'd been engaged in the tea trade when his ship had sunk in a storm, and it angered Connor to have the marchioness denigrate his memory.

"Actually, it was his devotion to both which led to his death," he said, fixing Lady Langwicke with an icy stare. "The earl was two steps from financial ruin before Adrian began 'gallivanting about,' as you called it.

The marchioness flushed an angry red, but the arrival of the tea cart kept the conversation from deteriorating any further. Talk became general after that, and when calm had been restored Portia decided it was time to take her leave. There was much she needed to do if all was to be ready for the last of the guests, and in any case, she wanted to get away from Connor's disturbing presence. His nearness was having a marked effect on her usual good sense, and she was anxious to leave before she did or said something that would make her love obvious to all.

She waited until he was deep in conversation with one of the younger men before taking the opportunity to slip quietly from the room. She thought she had made it until a firm hand closed about her elbow, pulling her to a halt on the other side of the door.

"Where are you going?" Connor asked, his voice soft as he gazed down at her.

She thought quickly, her mind seizing on her conversation with the marchioness. "I . . . I need to speak with the housekeeper," she replied, furious with herself for stammering. "If Mr. Granger is indeed the heir to an earldom, he really ought to have his own room. We shall have to reassign the rooms, and that will take some doing."

"I shouldn't bother." He dismissed the matter with an indifferent shrug. "If Granger doesn't care for his present quarters, he is free to bunk with the horses. Besides, I wouldn't be so quick to write off Adrian if I were you. If there was any way possible to have survived that shipwreck, he will have found it."

Portia did not bother with an answer. Rearranging Mr. Granger's accommodations had been a mere ploy, and having been deprived of that, she quickly thought of something else.

"As you say, my lord." She inclined her head politely, wishing he would take the hint and release her arm. "In that case, I will need to go up to the attic and check on the costumes I have arranged for some of our guests."

Her use of his title as well as her obvious determination to escape his company flicked his pride on the raw, and for a moment he was strongly tempted to pull her into his arms and kiss her senseless. Only the knowledge that such an action would stain her reputation beyond repair stayed him, and he reluctantly released her arm.

"Very well," he said, his jaw clenching as he fought for control. "Perhaps I will see you later then? There is another assembly this evening, and Mother insists that we all attend. Will you ride in our carriage?"

Until this moment Portia had fully intended to attend the local dance. But suddenly the thought of watching Connor waltzing with Lady Duxford was more than she could endure, and she knew she would have to cry off. "I am afraid not, your lordship," she said, her chin coming up as she faced him. "With the guests arriving on the morrow, there is much I need to do. But I hope that you and the others will have a wonderful time."

Her words, spoken in that cool, precise tone, made Connor flinch, and abruptly, he was reminded of his Season in London. It seemed that once again his attentions were unwanted. This time the knowledge shattered more than his pride. It shattered his heart.

He stared down at Portia, wanting to scream a denial of the pain clawing at him. He loved her, he realized dazedly, a love so great it reduced the emotions he had felt for Olivia to mere boyish infatuation. He wanted to marry Portia, and then carry her off to his room and make love to her until she admitted she was his. Her rejection of him was not so cruel as Olivia's, he thought bitterly, but it was just as painful ... and as final. Knowing she did not return his love, he knew he had no choice but to keep his distance from her. Somehow, he would have to keep his love to himself.

* * *

Over the next sennight Portia kept too busy to brood over the sad state of her heart. In between the dinner parties, picnics, and endless hands of whist and Pope Joan, she saw little of Connor, a situation helped by the fact that he seemed equally determined to avoid her. She tried telling herself it was for the best, but she would remember the closeness they had once shared, and she would mourn for what had been and what would never be.

Complicating matters was the letter she had received from her great-aunt, inviting her to join her in Scotland. The countess, it seemed, had decided to forgive her black-sheep niece her many failings, and was now demanding her presence at her side. Portia had told no one of the missive, but she knew the letter provided her with the perfect excuse to leave Hawkshurst should it prove necessary. Another deception, she thought with an unhappy sigh, wondering if the duplicity would ever end.

The afternoon prior to masquerade ball was surprisingly peaceful. While the guests rested for the festivities, Portia decided to go for a ride. It was a pleasure she had denied herself since the ill-fated trip into York, and as she rode over the green, rock-strewn hills, she knew she saying good-bye to the land she had come to love as much as she loved its owner.

She drew her horse up on the rise, tears filling her eyes as she gazed slowly about her. She would always carry the memory of the place and the man in her heart, and she knew she would never be able to look at the moors without remembering him. The thought brought a bitter smile to her lips. Finally, she mused, she was behaving like a true lady, starry-eyed and hopeless with love.

On impulse she decided to visit the old ruins, and nudged her horse in that direction. She'd almost reached her destination when she saw Connor and Lady Duxford standing by the stones. Even as she was absorbing this painful sight, the marchioness flung her arms about Connor and drew him down to her for a passionate kiss. Unable to bear the agony of it, Portia spun her mount around and galloped off, her eyes streaming with tears, and her heart shattering in her chest.

"Really, Connor, you disappoint me," Lady Duxford chided, her expression reproachful as she drew back from Connor. "I thought we understood each other."

"As did I, my lady," Connor answered coolly, his gaze hard as he studied her beautiful and calculating face. He had brought her to the ruins on purpose, determined to put his painful past behind him at last. It was a test of sorts, and he realized with satisfaction that he had passed with flying colors.

"I cannot believe you are still holding my rejection of you against me," Lady Duxford continued, a note of desperation stealing into her voice. "I told you, the choice was not mine! My parents insisted I marry Duxford. What else could I do?"

"Nothing."

The blunt reply made her blink. "I wanted to accept you," she insisted, laying her hand on his arm and gazing up at him with ardent longing. "You cannot imagine how painful it was to send you away. My poor heart was breaking, but Mama was adamant."

"Now it is you who disappoint me, Lady Duxford," he interrupted, his mouth twisting in a rueful smile. "But you are wrong to think I hold your refusal of my suit against you."

"Do you mean you do not?" From her expression Connor gathered she did not know whether to be relieved or offended.

"No. In fact, I feel quite the opposite," he said, smiling with cold pleasure. "Since meeting you again, I have been on my knees thanking the Almighty for my deliverance."

Lady Duxford's face turned an unbecoming shade of red, and she lashed out with her gloved hand. "Bastard!" she exclaimed, her eyes bright with fury. "You are as beastly and uncivilized as you always were!"

"Thank you, my lady." Connor gave her a mocking bow. "Fortunately for me, there is a certain lady who prefers beastly and uncivilized men. Now, if you have finished attempting to seduce me, it is time we were riding back. I've much to do."

"Well, you look a sight, I must say," Nancy muttered, hands on her hips as she studied Portia. "Did the ladies really wear them queer things?"

"According to Lady Eliza, they were all the crack some sixty years ago, although heaven knows how the poor creatures managed to get through the doorways." Portia's expression was dubious as she studied her reflection in the glass. "I look like a table that's decided to go exploring on its own."

Designed in rich red brocade and lavishly embroidered with gold and silver threads, the gown was a far cry from the modest and fashionable dresses Portia had always worn. Rather than the straight, graceful skirts she was accustomed to, the skirts on the ball gown extended a full sixteen inches on either side of her, making walking difficult and the thought of dancing laughable. The gown was also cut scandalously low, and Portia

was trying to decide whether or not she should
stuff another lace fichu in the neckline when
Nancy spoke.

"Mayhap it wouldn't look so odd if you was to
wear one of them powdered wigs," she suggested,
looking thoughtful. "I remember a grand lady
from my village used to wear one, and I thought
she looked like a queen."

Portia remembered the graying, vermin-invested
wig she had found along with the gown, and repressed a shudder. "No, thank you, Nancy," she
said, giving in to the desire for modesty and tuck-
ing a lacy fichu in the tight bodice. "I shall be uncomfortable enough as it is, and I much doubt
Great-aunt will thank me if I arrive at her home
infested with fleas."

The mention of the countess and the pending
move to Scotland made Nancy sniff with disapproval. "Don't know why we need to go tearing
off to her ladyship's," she grumbled, moving behind Portia to finish arranging her hair. "What's
wrong with this place, I'd like to know?"

Portia closed her eyes, remembering the sight of
Connor kissing Lady Duxford. "Nothing," she said
at last, her tone bleak as she opened her eyes to
gaze in the mirror. "Only that it is not our home,
and we mustn't impose on his lordship's kindness
any further. Now that Lady Doncaster has recovered from her injury, there's no reason to remain."

"Isn't there?" A secretive look stole across
Nancy's face. "If you say so, Miss Portia. But I do
wish you would reconsider; only remember what
happened last time you went calling on your
great-aunt."

Portia did, and it was all she could do not to
burst into tears. "It is different this time," she insisted, swallowing the urge to cry at the memory of
Connor towering over her. "Great-aunt Georgianne

has invited me, and you needn't make it sound as if we are making off into the night like a group of sneak thieves. I fully intend to inform Lady Doncaster of my decision tomorrow morning."

"And when it is you wish to leave?" Nancy pressed.

"By week's end," Portia said, giving her reflection one final look before turning away. "That will give you enough time to pack, won't it?"

Nancy handed her the ornate fan that completed the ensemble. "Oh, more than enough time, miss," she informed her with a cheeky grin. "More than enough time."

The grand ballroom of Hawkshurst had been transformed into a fairy woodland. After making her cautious way down the stairs, Portia paused to admire the result of her weeks of hard work. Baskets of white roses and bushy ferns from the countess's greenhouse were interspersed about the room with delicate gilt chairs and tables. She had to admit the effect was pleasing.

"There you are." A familiar voice sounded in her ears, and she turned to find Connor standing behind her. The sight of him dressed in the clothing of a Roman centurion drove the breath from her lungs. She gazed at him in amazement.

The expression on her face made Connor flush with embarrassment. He'd felt like a damned fool rigging himself out like this, but his mother had insisted he wear a costume. Given his only other choice was to don a toga and a headdress of olive leaves, he'd thought he'd chosen wisely, but now he wasn't so certain. When Portia continued staring at him, he shifted uneasily from one sandled foot to another.

"I wish you would say something, Portia," he

said, striving for a light tone. "These things are dashed uncomfortable, you know."

"No more uncomfortable than this," Portia replied, deciding that if he could act so nonchalant then so could she. "At least you can move without knocking over everything in sight."

He took in the elaborate dress with its massive side skirts and repressed a grin. "Actually, I think you look charming," he drawled, his eyes coming to rest on the neckline of the gown where she had arranged the fichus. "Although I think you could dispose of one of these," he added, running the tip of his finger across the rich lace. "Afraid of catching a chill?"

Her cheeks grew warm, and she rapped her fan against his hand. "It is interesting, don't you agree, how many of our guests have chosen costumes which resemble their true selves?" she asked, refusing to comment on his audacious behavior. "Look at your friend Mr. McLean, rigged out like a brigand, and there is Lady Langwicke dressed as Queen Bess. I always thought her far too regal for a mere marchioness."

Connor heard the nervousness beneath her chatter, and wondered what was troubling her. Now that he had at last made peace with his past he was ready to face his future, and he prayed he would be able to convince her to be a part of it. Taking a deep breath for courage, he reached out to take her hand. "Portia, there is something I wish to ask—"

"Speaking of marchionesses, will Lady Duxford be coming?" Portia asked, her smile falsely bright as she turned to him. "I am sure her costume will be most interesting."

"Olivia?" Connor's brow gathered in a frown at the interruption. "What makes you think she is coming tonight?"

"I . . ." Portia's voice trailed off at his question and she stared at him for a brief moment. "I assumed you had invited her, my lord," she said, ruthlessly smothering the small flame of hope that had flickered to life in her. "You have been seeing a great deal of her of late and—"

"There the two of you are," Lady Eliza exclaimed, limping heavily as she crossed the floor to join them. "I have been looking for you everywhere." She fixed Portia with a pointed glare. "And what is this I hear about you going to Edinburgh?" she demanded. "A fine notion of gratitude you have, to go sneaking off the moment my back is turned."

Portia felt the blood drain from her face, and then return so quickly her cheeks stung. She realized Nancy must have confided in Gwynnen, and Gwynnen, of course, had gone straight to her mistress with the tale. The private word she had hoped to have with the countess was now impossible, and aware that they were the object of several interested stares, she did her best to strive for something approaching dignity.

"I hadn't meant to abuse your hospitality, my lady," she said, thinking in a detached manner that she was conducting herself with all the grace and decorum her father might have wished for. "But my great-aunt has written requesting that I join her in Scotland and I—"

"Scotland!" Connor's roar threatened to shatter the panes of the wide French doors opened to let in a cooling breeze. "If you think you are going to Scotland, you are out of your bloody mind!"

The harsh words brought an immediate hush to the room, and the expression on his glowering countenance caused several young ladies to succumb to the vapors. Above the cacophony Connor could hear someone muttering something about "the Beast," but he was too furious to pay the words any mind. Instead he advanced on Portia, his hands clenched into fists.

"I have been patient long enough," he announced between clenched teeth, noting with pride that she didn't retreat so much as an inch. "I told myself I would respect your tender feelings, that I would not offer for you while I was uncertain of what you felt for me, but this is enough. You are going to marry me, Portia, and that is the end of it."

There were more gasps, and the sounds of even more ladies swooning, but Portia ignored them. She could not think clearly, and a terrible sense of panic began welling up inside her. She wanted so much to believe he meant the blunt declaration, but she was afraid. If he was offering for her because he was piqued with Lady Duxford, it would destroy her, and she would rather reject his offer out of hand than risk such a terrible pain. She flung back her head and sent him a furious scowl.

"As if I would marry an egotistical, overbearing tyrant like you!" she declared, infusing as much scorn as she could into the words. "And even if I was so foolish as to overlook your barbaric manners, I would never countenance your rakish ways!"

Connor had been accused of being many things, but never a rake, and he was temporarily at a loss how to defend himself. When he could think of no response, he impatiently brushed her heated charge aside. "Rake, or nay, I will marry you!" he said, reaching out to grab her hand. "Now stop complaining and come with me. We have a wedding to plan." And before she could protest any further, he began dragging her unceremoniously from the ballroom.

Portia fought, but between her cumbersome

skirts and Connor's fierce strength it was a useless struggle. The moment they were on the balcony he released her hand. She wasted little time in swinging her fist at his face. He dodged the blow easily, grabbing her hand and pulling her against him. His mouth closed over hers in a burning kiss, and at a touch of his lips the fight drained out of her. Her hands came up to his shoulders, clenching in the soft wool of his cape and pulling him closer.

"Portia." His voice was low and urgent as he plundered her mouth and the slender column of her throat. "I love you. How could you even think of leaving me?"

The husky words made Portia's legs go weak, and had Connor not been holding her so possessively, she would have collapsed at his feet. "You . . . you love me?" she echoed, her eyes wide as she studied his face. "Are you certain?"

"Of course I am certain," he replied with a husky laugh, the joy and disbelief in her voice telling him all that he needed to know. Not that he was satisfied, of course. He gave her another kiss, his tongue briefly tasting her sweetness before he raised his head again.

"And now don't you think it is time you told me you loved me?" he asked, his hands disposing of her fichu so that he could stroke the creamy flesh revealed by the gown's neckline.

She sighed under his daring touch, surrendering the last of her fears and doubts. "I do love you," she agreed, and then spoiled her act of sweet submission by adding, "Although heaven knows why. You are a beast, you know."

He grinned, barely able to recall the time when similar words had caused him pain. "So I am," he drawled, "and you are the furthest thing from a lady I have yet to encounter. Can you think of two people who deserve each other more?"

Portia thought about that for a moment, and then gave a low laugh. "No, I cannot," she said, linking her arms around his neck as she smiled up at him. "Now stop chattering like a foolish schoolboy and tell me what the devil you meant by kissing Lady Duxford this afternoon. If you think I'll tolerate such behavior once we are married, you may think again."

Connor laughed at her threat, bending to kiss her sulky mouth. He explained his need to put his childish infatuation with Olivia behind him once and for all, and he was not in the least surprised that she understood at once.

"I only wish I might have made a similar peace with my father," she said, leaning her head against his shoulder, her eyes misting as she thought of the past. "He was always berating me for my lack of ladylike qualities, but I think perhaps he would be proud of me now."

"I am sure he was always proud of you," Connor said. "I think it is the way with parents and children to squabble. Besides—" He slipped his hand beneath her chin and raised her face to his "—had you been a lady, you would never have hit me over the head with a bed warmer, and then we might never have found ourselves standing out here."

"That is so." Portia was delighted to think he approved of her hoydenish ways. She gave him another grin, but when he would have kissed her she drew her head back with a jerk.

"Just let that be a warning to you," she cautioned with a scowl. "Chase another pretty blonde into a bedchamber, and I'll do more than dent a bed warmer over your hard head. I trust I have made myself clear?"

"Quite clear, love," Connor said solemnly, then tried to gather her close. Her side skirts interfered, and he gave them an angry scowl. "Now I know why the damned things went out of style," he said. "The gentlemen of my grandfather's time wouldn't have tolerated such nonsense."

They continued kissing and making plans for their life together when the countess interrupted them. "If you have quite finished causing the scandal of the Season, do you think you might return to the ballroom to announce your engagement?" she asked in a sour tone, her eyes shining with satisfaction as she took in their mussed condition. "And kindly straighten your clothing; I'll not have people counting on their fingers when your son makes his appearance."

Both Connor and Portia blushed at such frank talk, but quickly followed her instructions. They were almost to the ballroom when Connor suddenly chuckled and pulled Portia to a halt.

"What is it?" she asked, gazing up into his face, her heart so filled with love it was a wonder it did not burst.

"I have just been thinking about your remark about costumes," he said, nodding at his mother's retreating back. "Do you not see how Mother is dressed?"

"Like a Grecian lady, I suppose," she said, unable to see his point. "But I—"

"Like the Oracle at Delphi," he corrected, laughing as he finally understood the way his mother had neatly been managing him. "All-knowing, and all-seeing, and very, very clever. Don't you see, my love? The wise old witch has outsmarted us all."

"And you do not mind?" Portia asked, thinking of the countess's cruel deception.

"So long as I have you, no." He bent and pressed a kiss to her mouth. "Although I do mean to have a word with her about the rig she has been running for this past year. That damned Bath chair cost a fortune."

Portia gave him a startled look, and then abruptly she too was laughing. They were still laughing when they entered the ballroom, much to the astonishment of those present. The Beast and the hoyden, it would be whispered for several generations to come, had tamed each other.